HARD TOWARD HOME

# HARD TOWARD HOME

STORIES

# C.D. ALBIN

Press 53
Winston-Salem

Press 53, LLC
PO Box 30314
Winston-Salem, NC 27130

First Edition

Cover design by Kevin Morgan Watson

Cover art, "Tim in Fog" Copyright © 2014 by Dawn D. Surratt, used by permission of the artist. instagram.com/ddhanna

Author photo by Kelli Albin

Printed on acid-free paper
ISBN 978-1-941209-34-9

*For my parents,*
*Mary Maxine Albin and Forest Porter Albin*

# Acknowledgments

Grateful thanks to the editors of the publications listed below for first publishing the following stories:

At Woods' Edge: *Cave Region Review*

The End of Easy Breathing: *Roanoke Review*

Four Fine Horses: *Crosstimbers* and *Yonder Mountain: An Ozark Anthology*

For You: *Red Rock Review*

Hard Toward Home: *Natural Bridge*

His to Give: *Rockhurst Review*

Judgment Call: *The Chaffin Journal*

The Price of Land: *The Arkansas Review*

Punch List: *Cave Region Review*

Traveling Mercies: *Cave Region Review*

# CONTENTS

We have one home, the first, and leave that one.
The having and leaving go on together.

—John Updike, "Shillington"

# HARD TOWARD HOME

L id McKee watched from his living room as Jessie Carrico parked her Buick inches from the grill of his pickup, then got out and opened the trunk. She was an old woman in dark slacks and a cream top, clothes she probably saved for trips to Jonesboro or Memphis, but now she leaned over the trunk and pulled out a pair of green rubber gloves. She put them on, grabbed a towel, and held it away from her until she reached the porch and saw him watching. She stopped and stretched her arm toward him, as if she thought he could step through the glass and take what she held.

Lid moved back from the window. He'd tried to talk her out of this, reminding her over the phone that his son was nearly thirty, grown and gone. Whatever trouble Reed got into was his own. But Jessie Carrico had a way. As a young teacher she had ruled the roughest boys in her seventh grade history class, Lid among them. He could remember the clipped cadence of her voice as she insisted, day after day, that each one could do better, be better. She'd sounded the same last month when he warned her not to rent Reed the little house in back of hers because Reed was liable to do anything for meth money, but she wouldn't listen. Now something had happened, and she was on his front porch, rattling the door as she knocked.

Lid stepped into the hall and saw her crowding the screen, her dull white hair drawn into a bun at the back of her head, her sharp face thrust forward as if she were glaring at a child. She poked the towel hard against the mesh. "That's your boy's blood. His blood on my towel. How you think it got there?"

Lid's throat felt dry. He stepped out and studied the cloth. "Are you hurt?"

"That's all his. There's more on my kitchen floor, a pool of it."

He squeezed the back of his neck where the muscles had bunched. "I warned you about him."

She started to speak, but changed her mind and shoved the towel into his hands. He felt the dampness, the thick, clinging weight of blood on his fingers. "There's nothing I can do," he said, and flung the towel to the end of the porch.

Her eyes never left him. "Not if you won't try."

He turned to go inside, but gloved fingers tightened on his arm and he fought to remain a man on a porch instead of a boy at Rock Valley School, a stone raised above a classmate's face. She had stopped him then too, prying the rock loose and slapping him once across the jaw. Now he pushed her hand away, but he remained on the porch. "Tell me what he did," he said.

A slow storm passed over her face. "He broke in through my sun porch. Dripped blood on my floors. I ran him off with a poker."

Lid focused on the stand of yellow pine across the road. The trees rose above a tangle of underbrush, and he wondered what cover Reed would seek now. "You see where he went?"

"He took off toward the rent house."

Lid looked at her.

"I checked," she said. "He's already gone."

Her bun had loosened, and a pale puff of hair floated near her temple. For the first time Lid noticed the blotchy patch of liver spots on her forehead. "You shouldn't have rented him that place. He don't know a debt."

She lifted her chin and frowned. "You won't give him a roof. I got a month's rent out of it."

"You got a thief in your kitchen."

"Your son in my kitchen."

He looked past her to the pines, but he could feel her eyes on his face, searching. "Do what you want. I'm done with him."

For a long time she didn't move. He noticed there was no wind in the tops of the trees. Finally she removed the gloves and dropped them at his feet. "I expect more of you," she said.

She went down the steps and started the Buick, backing hard into his yard. At the end of the drive, her brake lights barely flickered before she turned onto the road.

After the car passed out of earshot, he gathered the towel and gloves and carried them to the gully behind his house, where he heaved them away and watched them land on a pile of trash. The towel made a dark patch, maroon as a new bruise.

The next morning Lid rose slowly, his muscles still sore from the three days last week he'd spent in the logging woods. He hated to think of fifty-six as old, but he'd wear out soon if the shoe factory didn't start up again. Twenty years of piecework had made him softer than he'd known.

He stood at the sink and ate cold cereal, and when he heard muffled sounds at the back of the house, he felt no surprise. Reed had forced the same window twice in the last month. Raising the bowl chest high, Lid held it over the sink and dropped it, letting it clatter loudly in the basin. Then he stepped into the living room, where he could see down the hall and study the doorway of the back bedroom. "I can smell your stink," he said.

There was a queer, close stillness. He rocked onto the balls of his feet as if to shout across a distance. "I said I can smell your stink."

Finally Reed came out of his old room, his shoulders filling more of the hallway than Lid remembered. A dirty rag encircled one hand.

"I told you not to come back," Lid said.

"You told me a lot of things."

"Not one of them took, either."

Reed said nothing.

"You're not getting anything from me."

"I didn't ask."

"Then what are you here for?"

Reed scratched at his cheek, studied a bit of straw he found in his beard. "Call it child support. I come to collect."

Lid felt his arms go weak. He swung as hard as he could, but Reed hit him in the throat. Then he was on the floor, gagging, his forehead pressed against the hardwood. Reed's knee ground between his shoulder blades and Lid felt a quick, hard jerk as his wallet came free. He tried to roll Reed off, but a blow at the back of his head drove his face against the floor. He lay still and listened to the fading sound of tennis shoes as Reed moved away. The sound returned though, the soft, scuffling tread he had never known he knew, and Reed leaned close and said, "You're as weak as that old woman."

For several minutes Lid lay where he fell, his brain filling with an old memory of a bird that had flown against the front window and made a sound like a gunshot. He'd gone onto the porch to find a brown, quivering clump, the broken neck bent beneath the body. With a shovel he carried it to the gully and flung it away, watching the wings spread once as air forced a final wing beat. Then the bird came down on a pile of rocks.

Lid raised himself to his knees and shook his head, trying to clear away the image. What came to him was the thought of Jessie Carrico. Limping to the phone, he found her number and called, waiting through ten rings before replacing the receiver. When he looked out the window, his pickup was gone.

She lived a mile down the road, and as best he could, he ran. Slowly pines gave way to oak and hickory. After a half mile he topped a large hill and spotted Jessie's green Buick upended in the ditch, one tire blown and the front end puncturing the turf like a plowshare. He hurried downhill and stuck his head inside, but the car was empty. Tubes of hand cream and an empty eyeglass case were strewn along the floorboard, the keys still in the ignition.

He turned and tried to sprint. His shoulders hurt him badly and his breath grew short, but he made it around the last curve and saw a patch of white siding behind the cedars. Struggling toward it, he fixed his eyes on whiteness until he passed beneath the trees and stopped at the edge of the yard. From there he could see the open door and the darkness beyond, so he rushed up the path while on either side geraniums erupted in clots of red.

At the door he yelled her name and entered. "Jessie," he yelled again. He crossed the living room and stepped into the kitchen, where he saw her on the floor. She groaned and reached a feeble hand toward him. Then he saw the bruises already forming on her face and neck.

◆  ◆  ◆

Two days passed before he was allowed to visit her at the hospital. When they finally said yes, he walked in to see her swathed in white, the sheet pulled high under her chin. One bruise, dark as soot, bloomed at the corner of her mouth.

"This is the first they'd let me come," he said.

She studied him as if he were a column of numbers. He felt awkward and hurried to set the gift shop flowers beside her bed. When she said nothing about them he cleared his throat and focused his gaze on the corner of her pillow. "I wish I had some words," he said.

Slowly she brought one hand from beneath the sheet and found his forearm. Her voice was a rustle of dry leaves. "What put that inside him?"

Lid shut his eyes. "You need your rest," he said.

Her fingers tightened. "I've not said it was him."

"Ma'am?"

"You did this, as much as him. But I've not told. That's for you."

She held him until he used his free hand to break away. He made it as far as the door when he heard the voice again, strong enough to make him turn. "Euclid!" she said. "I'm asking you."

In his cousin's rusted Ford pickup, Lid left the hospital and drove seven miles down a narrow county road east of Lotten, its shallow ditches crowded by scrub oak and hickory. Occasionally a clearing opened on a rocky patch of yard and a small house or trailer set back against the tree line. He drove slowly, listening to wind through the open window and the crunch of tires on packed clay. Finally he crested a ridge and saw below the tarred road that ran past Rock Valley School. He braked and stared down at the empty schoolyard, the place where Jessie Carrico had kept him from killing a classmate.

That morning he was sitting in a back row when Jessie called his name. All week she had been summoning other students, two each day to go to the front and say what they knew about Arkansas or the Ozarks, or even Bond County. He never believed she would make him walk the narrow aisle between desks and turn to face the class, but that morning she did. He stood speechless long enough to hear laughter begin in the back corner and to see a girl on the front row nod to him, her bright bangs shining above blue, earnest eyes that made him want to speak, but his tongue was mute. Finally he lowered his head and stared at his boots, paralyzed by shame until Jessie Carrico gripped his shoulder. "We'll try again tomorrow," she said. "You go sit."

Afterward, near the ball field, he heard a quick rush from behind just before Carl Epley buckled his legs. He pitched forward and lay for a moment, burning under the same laughter as before. Then he grabbed a rock and smashed Epley's knee, dropping him to the ground. The boy yelled and tried to crawl away, but Lid scrambled after him, swinging for his head. He missed twice before Jessie caught him and wrested the rock away. She ordered him to the office, but he turned his back on her and walked straight into the woods, where cedar and sumac grew so thick beneath the oaks that she halted her pursuit and stood calling his name. He pushed on until her voice was no more than a splinter beneath the skin, a pain he felt only faintly and thought he could bear.

After that the woods became a habit he never thought of breaking, not even when he'd grown and started a family, but then he took the boy hunting the first time. Reed was only seven, and he complained constantly of cold, pleaded to be taken home. "Hush up," Lid told him, and when Reed kept talking he reached out and caught the boy by the mouth. He could feel the cold cheeks, the thin lips moving against his palm. He shook once, letting the force travel from his shoulder to his hand. When the small, dark eyes narrowed with rage, he tightened his grip, squeezing the boy's jaws until he could feel the delicate bone structure and see the willfulness fading from the eyes.

Moments later he watched as the ridge, the vague clumps of cedar and oak, finally even the buck emerged out of the gray morning. He raised the rifle, but Reed let out a gasp. Lid missed, then turned and struck Reed across the face. The boy keeled to one side and Lid stood stunned, astonished at himself. Stooping, he slung Reed over his shoulder and started out of the woods. By the time they neared the pickup, Reed had recovered enough to begin kicking him in the ribs, but he walked on, the boy's boots pounding his side so steadily that when he stopped and let the boy slide to the ground the pounding continued, a phantom assault against his lower rib.

The memory was vivid enough that Lid reached for his side, squeezing the soft flesh above his belt until the truck cab became real to him again. Then he ground the gears and let the truck roll down the hill to where the dirt road met the blacktop. At the crossroads he sat for a moment, thinking how his son had never stopped kicking, how this last blow-up had put Jessie Carrico in a hospital bed. The thought stung him so hard he spun the truck onto the blacktop and headed back toward Lotten and the county jail.

In the lobby he waited for ten minutes until a deputy motioned him down a hallway toward the sheriff's office, where he sat across the desk from Sterle Hollis, a graying, sharp-boned man with hooded eyes. "There's something I need to tell," Lid said.

Hollis leaned forward, resting his weight on his elbows. He nodded to Lid as if he had heard a truth. "I'm listening."

Lid took a tight grip on the armrests. "Reed McKee. You know who he is?"

"I sure do."

The light in the room seemed unnaturally bright. Lid closed his eyes. "My boy," he began, but his throat grew parched, his lips dry. Finally he willed the rest of it. "My boy. He beat Jessie Carrico."

In the days that followed, Lid turned down three offers for logging jobs. He stayed close to the house and listened to radio reports from the local station, never leaving home except to weed and water Jessie's vegetable garden. Finally an evening report opened with the news that Reed and several others had been arrested at a meth lab in the northwest corner of the county, near the Missouri border. Lid sat with his arms crossed for several minutes, slowly absorbing what he had heard. The newscast ended and a country music song warbled into the room. When the lead singer took up the chorus a second time, Lid switched off the radio and called the jail.

The dispatcher had a nervous voice. She put him through to Hollis, and Lid heard a tired sigh. "We got him a few hours ago," Hollis said. "He was cooking meth over in Raintree."

Lid rubbed his temple with the heel of his hand. "So what now? Is he all right?"

There was another sigh, slower than the first. "I'll tell you this. He's about as good as you could expect."

"What's that mean?"

"Mr. McKee, he thought he wanted to fight. But the ambulance boys looked at him, and nothing's broke. We've got him back here on a cot."

For a moment Lid felt like ripping the phone off the wall, but the anger passed quickly, replaced by something akin to grief—for Jessie, for Reed, perhaps even for himself. He heard Hollis ask if he was still there, then ask again. He nodded as he returned the receiver to its cradle. A moment later he wandered into the kitchen, where he sat down at the table and let the darkness grow around him. In time the vapor light came on outside, and he stared at the glow it made in the window above the sink.

His wife, Glenna, had stood at that window the night she told him Reed was too much for her to handle, that she had to find someone who could understand the anger in him and make it go away. The next morning she and the boy set out for Memphis. Lid let a week pass before he got in his truck and went after her, but somewhere between Trumann and Marked Tree he pulled off the road and stared at the bare, flat land. He'd left the hills behind an hour before when he crossed the Black River. Surrounded by the long, low sweep of cotton, he realized she would endure the city and its close walls, its thick air and alien clamor, just to be rid of him. The knowledge seared like a burn, and he swung the truck around and drove hard toward home.

He had no news for three years until a letter arrived from Glenna's second cousin. A house fire, the letter said. The boy had escaped, made it out fine, but Glenna had not. They were sending him the boy. Then on Reed's first night back, while the two of them sat together at the kitchen table and ate a silent meal, Lid noticed how Reed's neck and shoulders were thickening with muscle, how his hands were already wide and strong. As Reed raised a spoonful of soup, Lid felt the words coming. "You tell me! Tell me how you get out and she don't."

Reed lowered the spoon, and for a moment Lid stared into a drowning face. Then the spoon hit the cabinet and Reed raked anything he could reach from the table. Lid grabbed for him but Reed twisted away, falling against the refrigerator. He was on his knees when Lid caught him and tried to say he hadn't meant it, that he didn't need to know anything about Memphis, but Reed pushed him away and sat banging his head against the refrigerator until Lid left the room.

Recalling that now, Lid began to shake. His forearm trembled against the table's edge, and he placed one hand atop another until the tremors eased. After a while he left the kitchen and walked down the hall to his son's old room. He entered without touching the light switch, and when he reached the bed he lay down and pulled the pillow to his chest.

For three days Lid went to the jail and waited, but Reed refused to see him. On the fourth morning, when Reed finally wore down and consented to appear behind the glass, Lid caught his breath. Reed's hair was shorn to the scalp and his beard was gone, the stubble only a faint shadow over the mound of bruise that swelled his jaw. He slumped down and rolled his chair as far from the glass as the tiny cubicle would allow, then trained his eyes on a cinder block in the near wall.

Lid leaned close, clearing his throat into the round speaker hole. "Look at me," he said.

Reed turned enough to glare at the glass. His voice sounded as if it came out of a tunnel. "You set Hollis on me."

Lid searched the swollen face, wondering what remorse would look like if it flickered there. "Put that beside Jessie Carrico. What you did to her."

"I ain't talking to you about that."

"You better talk to somebody. That lawyer any good?"

Reed shook his head. "I'm not listening."

For the first time in years, Lid wanted to grip his son's shoulder, squeeze the back of his neck. Regret made him so tired he rested his forehead against the glass. "I should've done better with you."

Reed rolled his chair close and put a hand in front of Lid's face, the gesture sudden and obscene. "You see this?"

Lid jerked back. "I come here to help you. I'm trying to tell you things."

"What do you know that's worth telling somebody?"

"I know I ruined you."

A slow smile stretched the corners of Reed's mouth. "You've got a high opinion of yourself. I never knew you were there."

"I don't believe that."

"You wouldn't, would you?" Reed sat back and laughed, his voice fading as he rolled his chair away. He stood and pounded on the door, his shoulders shaking slightly with laughter. The door opened and he almost stepped through. Then he turned and leaned down to the speaker. "If you really feel so bad, why don't you buy me some cigarettes?"

On his way home, Lid debated whether to check on Jessie Carrico. She'd been back on her place a couple of days now, but he dreaded seeing her. He'd nearly decided not to stop when he noticed several mailboxes along the road were damaged, probably by kids with baseball bats. He slowed when he reached her lane. The white, hand-lettered box was deeply dented and twisted on its stand. Shaking his head, he turned in behind the cedars.

She didn't answer when he knocked, so he went around to the garden, where he found her hoeing a row of tomato plants. She looked shrunken somehow, brittle in the bright sun. "There's no sense you being out here," he said. "It'll hit ninety before long."

She spoke over her shoulder. "I'm just getting to these weeds."

"I thought I got'em already."

Straightening, she shielded her eyes from the sun, but didn't look at him. "I'm grateful."

"I can probably fix that mailbox too."

Her bun was loosely pinned, and he could see the points of her shoulders beneath her thin cotton shirt. "You ought to have a hat on."

"I'm about done."

She kept scratching at the ground and he followed, sometimes stooping for a stone and slinging it into the woods. Finally he reached around her and took the hoe. "Let me have this."

She stared at her palms. "Have you been to see him?"

"I just come from there."

The words made her flinch, as if they brought Reed too near. "I heard he was hurt," she said.

"He was."

She clenched her eyes, her face ashy as old barn wood. He wondered if she still cared about Reed, or if she just wanted to forget her own hurt. "It don't matter what they give him," he said. "He'd deserve it. I would too."

When her eyes came open, their bright clarity startled him. He looked away at the cedars near the road, at the pale geraniums leading to her house. He'd not remembered to water them, or her yard either, where brown patches were forming like scabs on skin. "I been trying," he said. "He won't talk to me."

She pulled two tomatoes from a vine, redness filling each hand. "You went. That's something."

Lid remembered Reed's laughter, those shoulders hunching up and down. "Waste of time, probably."

Her thumb traced a circle around a green stem. "So much is."

She sounded tired, and Lid felt the full heat of noon. He searched his memory for a sign that good could follow after bad, but there was nothing, just the time or two he'd seen a sun-scorched plant sprout from the root. "You don't think there's any way?" he asked.

She studied him, sifting him with her eyes. Finally she set the tomatoes on his palm. "I don't hold a hope," she said, then squeezed his wrist. "But I've been wrong before."

# At Woods' Edge

L auren had heard no rifles since early morning, when three loud reports startled her from sleep and Robert pulled her close, growling "It's only hunters" in her ear. Yet the blasts jangled her nerves, made her feel out of step from the start. At breakfast she couldn't collect herself, absent-mindedly grabbing milk from the refrigerator when she meant to pour juice and putting a large slab of margarine on the same dish as the strawberries. Somehow she also managed to neglect the coffee, which meant Robert had to leave for rounds at the hospital without his morning jolt. From the front window she had watched him surge away, the scoot of the Camry's tires sounding to her like a small, petulant rebuke.

Now she sat at her desk and studied the long, sloping backyard, the cut-over hayfield and the thick gray woods beyond. She'd been wrestling with a freelance piece on gardening in the Ozarks, hoping to place it with a lifestyle magazine she'd seen out of Little Rock, but she couldn't bring anything into focus, every line dead with cliché. This region was native to Robert, not her. After twenty-four comfortable years in Ladue he'd suddenly been seized by the urge to return to Arkansas and re-root, taking over as head of the oncology unit in his hometown's only hospital. The quickness of his decision had stunned her, and with equal quickness she had come to think of Lotten not as a town but a mistress, another woman for whom Robert might well leave.

"You're selfish," she told him that morning four months ago, before the move. "We've made a life here."

Sitting on the edge of the bed, he tied one shoe, then the other. "We can do more in Lotten."

"More?"

"You know how much that town needs."

"You don't have to be the one to give it."

He let out a sigh she thought would empty his lungs, so long and slow she remembered the three miles he ran each morning. "It's home," he said.

Home to her was St. Louis, not this fieldstone house set on a ridge so deep in the woods their nearest neighbors were cattle farmers who lived half a mile away. On days like this, alone and brooding, she couldn't keep her eyes from the endless trees encircling the house. Robert loved the privacy, but she felt walled in.

Her one release was the tractor trail, an old path that began behind the eyesore of a barn they were yet to raze and ran along the west side of the property. Robert ran the trail each morning, and she had taken to hiking it whenever she felt overly confined within the house. Yet she'd avoided it the last week or so, fearing some careless hunter crouched in the woods might mistake her for a deer. When she told Robert of her concern he had merely laughed, pointing her to the bright orange vest he'd donned for runs since the opening of the firearms season. She supposed it would keep her safe too.

From the closet she grabbed a faded denim jacket and pulled the vest over it, feeling garish and swallowed by fabric when she looked in the mirror. All she needed to complete the outfit was one of those camouflage caps she'd seen country people wearing in town. Even some women wore them. She went out through the finished basement and stood for a moment on the back patio, taking in what she thought of as the close sky, closer than anything she could remember in Ladue, gray cloud-scud hanging low over undulating tree lines.

To her right the barn loomed like a monolith of sagging clapboard, its missing front doors yawning into a dark tunnel that opened again at the back of the barn where the trail began. Always before she had walked around the barn to get to the trail, but now she shoved her hands deep into the pockets of the vest and moved toward the structure, noting blotches beneath the eaves where remnants of paint had faded to the maroon of dried blood.

She had been inside the barn only once, when the real estate agent showed them the property. At the time, Robert had remarked on the old tools left behind by former owners. He thought some of the tools might be cleaned up a bit and displayed, or perhaps sold to an antique dealer, but so far he had done nothing with them. Now Lauren studied a couple of rusty hooks and guessed they might have been used to carry hay bales. To her they looked like props from a bad horror film. Who would buy such things, she wondered.

Beyond the barn the trail led her out to the edge of the property and turned south, taking her down through the field that separated the yard from the woods. Come spring, she meant to turn that jumbo-sized yard into a garden, one with a semblance of scale and proportion, but for now she felt no strength even to plan the task. Instead she gazed on the acres of pasture and imagined some farmer at his own labor, tossing out hay or feed while cattle made their slow way from the pond.

Suddenly Lauren spotted a movement at woods' edge. Straining her eyes, she scanned the blank gray trunks of trees until a downed doe, head and neck raised, became clear against the backdrop. At first Lauren thought the doe might be nursing a fawn, but then she remembered Robert telling her the birthing season would end in May, June at the latest. She stepped off the trail and walked slowly toward the center of the field, waiting to see if the doe would rise and bolt. When it didn't, she angled her path so that she could approach the deer in a straight line. Drawing closer, she could tell it was watching her, its ears twitching to her footsteps as she strode across the dry stubble, but the deer remained on the ground, placid as a pet dog.

Wondering if the animal had been shot, she waved her arms, thinking motion might startle it to its feet. When it didn't move, Lauren studied the ground, noticing that even in a cut-over field like this one loose stones lay strewn across the surface. Selecting one that filled her palm, she went still closer and lobbed the stone underhanded. Her aim was good, the rock falling a few feet from the deer's rump and rolling past. At the thud, the doe turned her head slightly before looking back at Lauren. This time Lauren judged the eyes vacant—still capable of sight, but absent of all interest.

Pulling out her phone, she walked back to the trail and dialed Robert's number, which sent her to voice mail. She hung up. The doe wasn't even looking at her now. After a minute, she dialed Robert again. "I know you're busy, but call as soon as you get this. It's important."

Returning to the house, she wasted a half hour Googling anything she could think of regarding deer behavior, but nothing came close to answering her questions. The frustration left her feeling as edgy and off-key as the time she'd downed an energy drink out of a vending machine. To set herself aright she went to the kitchen and began to brew a cup of green tea when the phone rang. "What's wrong?" Robert demanded, his voice hurtling through the receiver.

She hadn't thought about how she would explain herself. "There's a doe at the edge of the woods," she said. "It won't get up."

"What?"

"There's no blood, Robert. If she'd been shot I should see blood, shouldn't I?"

There was silence. Then a muffled curse. "Lauren, if you're not the one bleeding, I don't have time. Call Game and Fish, okay? Maybe they'll talk to you."

"I'm sorry. I know you're busy."

"I have a nine-year-old with a tumor behind the eye. Okay?

"Okay."

He ended the call before she could say goodbye.

Afterward the house seemed thick with silence, as if the sound of her breath took up space the quiet claimed by right. Still holding the phone, she gathered her jacket and vest from the couch where she'd tossed them and went out to the front porch. She rested her forehead against a column and wondered what it would have been like growing up here. Robert rarely spoke of his childhood, which he'd spent shuffling between his father's farm at the south end of Bond County and his mother's house in town. Both properties had been sold more than a decade ago, but Lauren thought now of Sylvia's house, that tiny rock cottage latched somehow to a soaring hill overlooking the rest of Lotten. She remembered looking out the front window one afternoon, wondering what kept the place from tumbling downhill like a runaway boulder.

"Nothing comes while you're watching," Sylvia had said from the kitchen doorway.

Lauren shrugged, tapped the window with her forefinger. "You must feel like you live on a ledge."

"Not really. Most of town's just in a valley." Sylvia came to the window. "Look across. You can see the old train station on the other side."

It was true. In the distance the horizon rose to level, a handful of buildings pockmarking a mass of green. "Our first vacation, Robert and I went to Mount Judea," Lauren said. "It was like this."

Sylvia nodded. "You could always go back. It's a short drive from here."

Below, one side of the square was visible through the trees, buildings laid out as evenly as a board game. "You know your son."

"Sometimes you have to take a man by the hand."

Lauren stepped away, sat down in the corner armchair. "Did Lowell like being taken by the hand?"

Sylvia sucked in her cheeks, her chin jutting. After a moment she smoothed her apron. "I believe we were best when I did."

From somewhere in the woods a lone bird called, and Lauren pushed herself away from the porch column. Even now, years after Sylvia's passing, she regretted the question. She had meant the words to wound, and Sylvia had known.

Descending the steps, Lauren called Information for the number of the local Game and Fish office, where an officer named Rodney Coldiron listened while she stumbled through her story.

"Okay," he said when she finished. "What is it you'd like me to do?"

"Can't you come out and check her?"

"It sounds like she probably needs to be put down. Do you have a rifle?"

"No," Lauren said. "I've never shot anything in my life."

She heard a rustle, as if the officer were shifting the phone from one ear to the other. Then came a sigh. "All right," he said. "If you'll give me directions, I'll head out your way."

Lauren searched her mental map of Lotten, placing the Game and Fish office on a wide knoll across the railroad tracks, near the end of Jefferson Avenue. If Coldiron left immediately she shouldn't have to wait more than fifteen or twenty minutes. Quickly she told him what county road to turn on and where to find the tractor trail once he arrived, then she buttoned her vest and set out, this time avoiding a pass through the barn. The whole way she contemplated the probable result of her call, what Robert would surely pronounce a mercy.

Entering the field, she saw at once that the doe had not moved. Resigned, she walked to the middle of the field and knelt, resting on her knees. How long, she wondered, had the animal lain there at the edge of the woods? Surely she couldn't have walked the trail yesterday and not seen the doe. Had she managed to spot something that Robert, with his country eyes, had missed?

Gradually Lauren sensed the wind lift, felt it advance in small, chill buffetings out of the southwest that she likened to the cautious, stalking steps of some predator, perhaps one of those coyotes she'd begun to hear yipping in the night. Her legs were growing stiff so she rose and stamped her feet to encourage blood flow. Finally, between gusts of wind, she caught the sound of a truck engine laboring in low gear.

By the time she made it back to the trail the officer had found a place to park at the edge of the field. He leaned out the window and followed Lauren's arm where she pointed. "That'd be her," he said.

"Yes."

Coldiron was a big, blond man in his early thirties who touched the bill of his cap as he stepped down from the running board. "Let's see if we can spook her," he said, then reached back into the cab and sounded several long, loud blasts of the horn. The doe turned her head toward the truck, but made no other motion. "I see what you mean," he said.

"I've no idea how long she's been there."

"Hard to know. You own this land, I guess?"

"Yes. And the woods . About twenty acres in woods, I think."

"Probably heard a few hunters this week."

"Every morning."

"Good spot for it," Coldiron said, and pointed toward her vest. "I like seeing that orange."

Lauren thrust her hands deeper into her pockets. "What will you do," she asked. When the officer looked toward the woods she stared, trying to make him turn back and hold her eyes.

Instead he studied the doe in the distance. "Probably she's not been shot," he said. "She'd be struggling more if that was the case. Surely."

"You'll examine her?"

"As best I can."

Lauren glanced at the truck. She saw no rifle mounted in the cab, but Coldiron wore a powerful looking pistol on his hip. His right hand rested on the gun butt. "I hope you give her every chance," she said.

Coldiron lifted his cap, ran thick fingers through yellow bristle. "I will," he said, "I assure you." He resettled his cap and, at last, found her eyes. "If you want, ma'am, you can go back to the house now. I promise I'll stop on my way back and let you know."

His tone was softer than she expected. She found herself wondering whether she and Robert should have had a son, and whether their son would have used that tone. Studying Coldiron's jowled, bland face, she nodded assent.

When she returned to the house, Lauren did not go in. The porch was furnished with rocking chairs and a wicker bench, but she huddled on the top steps, arms wrapped around her legs and her chin tucked to her knees. At her feet lay a pile of blown leaves, mostly pin oak, some already brittle enough to rattle in the breeze. She closed her eyes and waited, hoping for the rumbling groan of Coldiron's truck, but the flat report of the firearm came first. She flinched, once, hugging her legs so tightly her forearms eventually grew fatigued. Massaging them, she stood and walked to the end of the drive to wait for Coldiron.

When he pulled up, he was already leaning out the window. "I guess you heard."

"Yes."

He removed his cap, tossed it on the dash. "It was tumors in her throat. They get them sometimes. She'd have starved if you hadn't called."

Lauren felt a thickening in her own throat. She never knew what to make of solace, or its strange semblances. Reaching up, she patted Coldiron's arm. "Thank you for coming."

"Not a problem." He put the truck in gear before leaning out again. "I drug her back into the woods a couple yards. That way you won't have to see her."

She nodded, raised a hand as he rolled down the drive.

Hours later Lauren watched from the living room as Robert returned home. To make up for the botched breakfast she had pulled together a version of his favorite lasagna and opened a bottle of Merlot, but when he entered he barely mumbled a greeting before crossing to the study and shutting the door. Lauren pondered whether she or a patient, perhaps the tumored child, was responsible for his mood. She let a few minutes pass before going back to check on him. She found him at his desk.

"Hungry?"

He shook his head.

"Try a bite or two. You'll find your appetite."

He shifted in his chair. "Maybe later. I'm pretty tired right now."

"Do you want me to keep it warm for you?"

"Please."

At the kitchen island Lauren ate a small plate of the lasagna and drank two glasses of wine. Putting the dishes away, she heard Robert cross to the bedroom. Moments later she heard the shower. She left the rest of the lasagna warming in the oven and tried to force a few sentences for the gardening article, but with no luck. Shifting to the couch, she turned on the television and stared at the images, oblivious. When Robert came in she handed him the remote, watched him flip back and forth between a news channel and ESPN.

"Are you going to eat anything?" she asked.

"In a bit."

"It's lasagna."

He flipped to C-SPAN. "No Book TV?"

"That's only on weekends."

Robert lowered the volume. "So what happened with the doe?"

Suddenly Lauren felt freighted by fatigue. She thought about the carcass in the woods, the tumors stopped by death.

"Did you call Game and Fish?" Robert asked.

She thought about Officer Coldiron. She wondered what to say about the color of his hair.

"Lauren?"

"I shouldn't have bothered you," she answered. "The doe went away."

Lauren woke gradually, drawn toward alertness by high, insistent cries. Fumbling with the alarm clock, she read 2:13. Beyond the window a chorus of yips surged sharply before beginning to fade. She sat up. Robert never seemed bothered by the coyotes. She wondered how he could have slept through these, so close to the house.

Easing out of bed, she went to the window. At first she could only see darkness, but after a while her eyes adjusted and she thought she could make out the darker mass of woods in the distance. The doe would be there, drawing creatures to her, if not tonight then soon. Lauren thought of the coyotes and their constant hunger, of bears not yet denned for winter. A few weeks ago she had watched a bobcat cross from one side of the yard to another, its carriage somehow arrogant, defiant, and she had withdrawn to the middle of the house, away from windows.

Now she looked to the bed where Robert lay on his side, the duvet turned back at his bare waist. Quietly she advanced, mounting the mattress on hands and knees, conscious of her weight and the noisy contractions of the springs. On all fours she lowered her body next to his, brushing his neck and throat with her lips. When he did not wake, she let her hand slide down the inside of his thigh. He startled slightly, rolled his top shoulder toward her. He spoke her name as if it were a question.

She cupped him, softly, before feeling his fingers close around her wrist. "Let's wait," he said. "I have early rounds tomorrow."

Robert rolled away, settling himself near the edge of the bed. For a few moments she listened to his breathing, heard it lengthen into deeper respirations of sleep. Within her she sensed a long pang, not hunger but fear of hunger. Reaching, she grasped his shoulder and drew herself to him. When he again tried to pull away she gripped him tightly, let her fingernails sink as he flinched.

# The Price of Land

Glen Green pressed his shoulders flat against the chair as April's father glared at him from the head of the table. Glen hated the way the older man could make him feel as light and rootless as straw. If it weren't for April he would have walked out ten minutes ago, but she'd found his hand beneath the table, and he could feel the tiny stone of her engagement ring grazing his knuckle. He squeezed her fingers, then looked straight at her father and held the man's stare. "That place," Glen said. "It's what I've got left."

John Lowe let out a long breath. His dessert plate was heaped with apple pie, but he pushed it away. "I named you a fair price."

"I never asked for one."

"Then what'll you do for money?"

"I got a job. Forty hours a week."

Lowe gripped the edge of the table as if he meant to overturn it. "You've got forty shares of nothing. Come December, you won't make the taxes."

Glen glanced at Mrs. Lowe, who had sealed her lips in a crease. Behind her the wind moved in the side yard, drifting dry leaves across the lawn. He released April's hand. "It ain't your worry," he said.

Lowe struck the table so hard coffee leapt from his cup. "Somebody better worry. There's a baby inside her."

"I said I'd support her. The baby too."

"Tell me how? You're nineteen. You don't even have a diploma."

Glen felt April's hand on his shoulder. He brushed it away and shoved himself from the table. When he turned back, her face was flushing. "Can't you say anything?" he shouted. "What happens to you inside this house?"

She shrank away as if he'd struck her, then her eyes widened and he knew before he turned that John Lowe was rising. He tried to hold the man off, stiff-arming him in the chest, but Lowe was too strong. He hooked Glen around the neck and dragged him backward down the hall, through the front door and onto the porch. Glen struggled to brace himself before his head cracked against a porch column and Lowe's forearm rammed beneath his chin, cutting off his air. "My house, you little tomcat," Lowe shouted. "She lives in my house. Don't you raise your voice to her."

Glen tried to knee Lowe in the groin, but Lowe caught his leg and tumbled him over the railing into the flowerbed below. He landed badly and fire seized his spine like a jolt from a cattle prod. For several moments he lay still, staring at a blank strip of sky between the porch roof and the maple tree. Faint voices seemed to hover there, until one swooped down and burst inside his ear. "Let me go," he heard April scream. "You hurt him. Let me go."

The back of Glen's neck had tightened like a vise, but he got to his feet and found the porch steps. Above him, April was straining to break her father's grip while her mother stamped one foot and shouted, "April. April, listen to me."

Glen started to charge the steps, but as he grabbed the railing he thought of the child April carried—the close quarters on the porch and the long drop to the ground. Lowe's broad face was still fierce, the neck tendons taut, bulging. "Wait now," Glen said. "Just let me talk to her."

"I already heard how you talk to her."

Glen took a deep breath, then straightened his shoulders and nodded. "Back there, that came out wrong."

"You said what you meant."

"No. I didn't mean to yell. But April and me, we've got to talk."

Glen held April's gaze for a moment, then watched her twist in her father's grasp and jerk one arm free, holding it in the air as if she might strike.

"You're not leaving with him," Lowe said to her.

"I'm not leaving with anybody. We'll just walk to the end of the drive." When Lowe hesitated, she stamped her foot like her mother. "His truck's right here. We can't run off."

Lowe's face darkened, but he gave in. "Twenty minutes," he said to Glen. "You have her back."

Glen nodded as April hurried down the steps to him. She slid her arm around his waist as if he needed support, and they walked a quarter of a mile without speaking, the only sound the crush of pea gravel beneath their feet. After they rounded the first long bend in the drive, April led him to a wrought-iron settee and made him sit so that she could rub his neck and shoulders. "You make him so angry," she said.

"I told you. I'm not selling him my land."

"You could listen at least. He wouldn't get so mad if he thought you were listening."

"Then why don't he listen to me? Rachel got the house. The land's the only thing in my name."

"But he can do something with it, Glen."

"You don't think I can?"

She didn't answer. Her hands left his shoulders and she slumped beside him, pouting the way she did when she wanted to be someplace else. He reached down and pried a half-buried walnut from the ground. The hard shell felt good on his fingertips as he rolled it back and forth. "If my sister won't sell the house, I'll get us a trailer," he said. "We can set it out there by the creek."

She stayed silent. The wind lifted, sending leaves streaming from the trees. "Out there under that big sycamore," he said. "You remember?"

"I've not said I'll do that."

Glen stood, walked away from the bench. A lone dogwood fronted the rest of the woods. He fired the walnut into a clump of ocher leaves. "You too good for a trailer?"

"We can do better than that."

"If I sell, you mean."

She slapped both knees hard. "We can get a house in town, Glen. Or out in Lake Haven. It's pretty there."

He retraced his steps until he could see around the bend. Her father's house loomed on the hilltop, white columns lined like sentries before a brick façade. "You're spending money I ain't got."

"You can get it. Most of it. Daddy'll help with the rest."

He shook his head. "We can't afford anything in Lake Haven. And we're sure not taking money from him."

The wind gusted again. She held her hair back from her face. "You better think about your baby."

"That's exactly who I'm thinking about."

"I wonder."

Glen jammed both hands into his pockets and made a fist around his keys. "I wonder what you meant when you said yes to me."

◆    ◆    ◆

He was surprised to see his sister's beat-up Cavalier parked near the porch when he arrived home. He stared at the plates for a moment, trying to guess why she hadn't moved farther away than Texas. When their mother left, she caught a bus in Jonesboro and rode all the way to California.

The light was on in the kitchen, where he found Rachel at the table with a cup of coffee. She wore a tight *Hard Rock* T-shirt and faded jeans. "Didn't know you were coming," he said.

"You never turn on the machine."

She reached out to hug him. He leaned down and let her squeeze him, briefly resting his chin on her shoulder. In the refrigerator, he found she'd stocked new lunch meat, soda, a six-pack of Lone Star beer. Popping one of the cans, he downed half before shutting the refrigerator and looking at her. "Your tires are worn," he said. "You need to rotate them."

"You sound like Daddy."

He studied her face, which was fuller now that she was in her twenties. Her hair was fuller too, dyed a harsh shade of gold that reminded him of Dallas, where she now lived. In May he'd spent a week at her apartment and never made peace with the bright, foreign glare of the Texas sun or the shining glass buildings he'd seen when he first arrived. He'd searched all week for a view that would rest his eyes, and when he drove out of the city, he wondered how she could stay there and not miss the close, wooded hills of the Ozarks. "How come you're back?" he asked.

She went to the sink and poured out her coffee. A tattoo of intertwining roses climbed one wrist. "I got a call," she said. "John Lowe."

Glen tensed. "The land's mine. I can do what I want."

His sister gave him a look of disbelief. "That's your biggest worry? That's the first thing you think about?"

"Sell me this house," he said, the words coming far sooner than he intended.

"What are you talking about?"

"Sell it to me. I'll borrow against the land."

Rachel laced both hands on top of her head. "God, how far along is she?"

He shook his head. "Four months. I figured he told you."

For a moment she studied him, then dropped her hands and turned to the window. Her face sagged, and Glen caught a vision of her profile at forty. Suddenly the room seemed too small. He slung open the screen door and went to the end of the porch. The sun was sinking, the sky above the barn going red and gold. In a few hours he'd be stuck at ArkMo, stamping bottle caps all night.

The door springs creaked and Rachel stepped out, letting the door clap against the casing. She lit a cigarette and rubbed her forehead with the heel of her hand.

"I can get a loan," Glen said.

"I don't think that'll work."

"There's eighty acres in my name. They'll lend me money."

With a fierce flick she sent the cigarette over the porch rail. "I've already got a buyer. He'll pay me twice, three times what you can borrow."

Glen felt his blood rush. He clamped her by the arm, shaking her. "What are you trying to do to me?"

Rachel stepped back and jarred him as she brought a hand across the bridge of his nose. "You prick. Daddy left this to me."

Glen blinked back the moisture that came with the pain. "Not if he'd known, he wouldn't have."

"I never said to hide it. Anyway, I'm quitting."

His mind flashed on her tiny apartment in Dallas, the strung-out strippers who swung by at any hour. From what he'd seen, they had been her only friends. "Who you promising?" he said.

She scowled at him. "Me, maybe. Surely not you."

"Surely."

She started back in, but stopped. "Why do you want this place, anyway? It's about to fall down."

"What do you care?"

"Just tell me."

He could feel the porch railing against his hips, reminding him of the fall at Lowe's. "She don't want a trailer," he said. "I need something more."

"And you think she'll stay here? For a week, maybe."

"She'll stay with me."

"God, Glen. Wake up."

He felt his face flush, a warm tingling that spread from his ears to the back of his neck. "What do you know about staying? How many of those cowboys stuck with you?"

She came close and poked a stiff finger in his chest. "I know this. You can ruin yourself before you get started. I've seen that plenty."

"I bet you have."

She nodded to him. "You'd win that one."

He waited until she left the porch and shut herself in her room before he went back in and made himself a sandwich. He barely finished half, then threw it away and stretched on the couch, where he tossed fitfully till time came to start for ArkMo.

At eight o'clock the next morning, Glen left the plant with the rest of the third shift and squinted against the sunlight, brooding that Lowe had offered Rachel so much money for the house. He drove straight to the Super 8 Motel and parked on the west side of the lot, where he watched a backhoe bite into a ridge on the far side of the bypass. The machine shaved off the crown and a clump of volunteer saplings, while at the base of the ridge two dump trucks hauled crushed limestone from John Lowe's new gravel pit. The land joined Glen's at the south end, and he imagined a layer of dust settling like soot all over his property.

On the way home he rubbed his emotions raw by telling himself Rachel had betrayed him, but when he pulled into the drive her Cavalier was gone. Instead of going in, he followed the unpaved farm road through two empty, weed-choked pastures and finally stopped beside the creek. Even his eyeballs felt tired, so he hung his legs out the door and tried to sleep in the cab, but the sun was too bright. Annoyed, he propped his weight on one elbow and stared over the dash. The sycamore loomed in front of him, ashy-white and nearly bare of leaves. He ran his eyes up to the strange vee where a twister had torn the top out years ago. A new lead branch had formed, but the sycamore would never be a pretty tree.

Staring into the broken canopy, Glen wondered why he had urged this place on April. The ground was flat enough for a trailer, and when the tree was in leaf there would be good shade, but for most of the year the creek was nothing but a long spill of gravel that snaked across the farm. Back in high school he'd trained for cross country by chasing the dry bed, but he hadn't run in over a year. He'd quit the day the principal and a highway patrolman called him out of class and told him his father had been crushed by a semi. That same morning Glen had braked at the end of the drive and glanced toward the barn, catching a glimpse of his father as he passed in profile, a feed sack hunched over his near shoulder. The Cardinals cap had been visible, but not his face as he disappeared into the barn. For nights after, Glen lay awake and thought of the lank body stepping through, the red cap never quite swallowed in darkness.

Now he eyed the misshapen sycamore and wished the twister had taken it whole. He knew Lowe would cut that tree, raze the house and barn, anything that said a Green once held title to the place. Eighty acres was too much land for a mall, but Lowe owned quarries and gravel pits all over north Arkansas. If he ever got hold of the farm, it wouldn't be worth seeing again.

In the early afternoon, Glen woke in his own bed, sunlight pouring through a crack in the blinds. Rolling over, he buried his face in a pillow until he heard someone moving downstairs. He lurched out of bed and grabbed his father's old .45 from the bureau before he remembered Rachel had spent the night. Cursing, he replaced the gun and pulled on his jeans.

Downstairs, Rachel was mopping the living room floor, working hard to brighten the dull pine. She gave him a wary nod, but Glen went straight to the kitchen, where he noticed the counters had been scrubbed, the floor mopped and polished. In the refrigerator he found part of a pizza, but after a few bites he tossed what was left in the box.

When Rachel came in, she shook her head at him. "This place was filthy. How could you stand it?"

Glen met her eyes. "You sold to Lowe," he said.

At first she crossed her arms, then pulled out a chair and sat down. "I don't have the money yet."

"It's him though, ain't it?"

"What if it is?"

"You know he'll force me off."

She rubbed her temples as if she had a headache. "I'm getting what I can, Glen. You should too. The price of land is rising."

"That's crap," he said, waving her words away.

"No, it's not. You've got a baby to pay for, and they'll make sure you do."

"April's not like that."

"You wait. You'll see."

"What will I see?"

Her words were slow, measured. "Glen, you're something she's sampling. She'll never marry you."

He noticed the sharp scent of Lysol on her clothes, saw dirt smudged below her left eye. "You just keep scrubbing," he told her. "You like his money so much, maybe he'll hire you to mop his floors."

She sighed, placed her hands flat on the table. "I'm through mopping. I'm going home. To Texas."

Three hours later, Glen sat in the Walmart parking lot hoping April wouldn't be late. On the phone she'd been reluctant to say she would meet him at all, insisting she was driving to Memphis to see her sister and didn't have much time. He'd told her he had to talk, couldn't get his head clear without her, and finally she agreed to swing by the parking lot on her way out of town.

He wasn't sure what he wanted to say, though a vague notion was forming. He thought maybe he could change her mind about Memphis. He had a blanket on the seat beside him, and he wanted to take her someplace where he could stretch out with her in the truck bed, maybe watch the sky darken to night and feel her body molding to his.

Suddenly the passenger door swung open, surprising him. April stared at the blanket on the seat. "What's that for?"

He shrugged.

"I told you I'm going to Memphis."

"I thought maybe we could drive over to Mammoth. Have a picnic or something."

"No."

Her face seemed strained, pale. He put the blanket out of sight behind the seat. "Get in, at least? We ought to talk."

"When I get back from Jenna's."

"Give me ten minutes."

She shook her head. "I'm late, Glen. I'll call when I get back."

Glen felt his throat tightening. "Maybe I could think about Lake Haven," he said.

She took a step back, far enough that he couldn't reach her. By the time he slid across the seat she was already in her car, the door locked. He struck her window with a flat palm. "April!"

She stared straight ahead while he stood beside her car shouting her name. Finally she lowered the window. "Next week, Glen. Right now I can't say yes or no."

"You already said yes."

"Don't do this."

"He's making you, ain't he?"

She shook her head in disgust and started the engine, racing it before she put the Saturn in gear. When he reached for the keys she slapped his hand away and spun out of the parking lot, nearly clipping the fender of a bread truck as she accelerated onto the highway.

His first instinct was to chase her, but by the time he bullied the truck into gear his mind had already locked on her father. He pushed the truck to top speed, its worn frame vibrating as he drove toward Lowe's gravel pit.

At the work site he roared onto the access road, a dust cloud filling his rearview as he slammed through ruts and potholes, twice grazing his head against the cab roof. Skidding to a stop in front of Lowe's office trailer, he came out of the truck so quickly his footing gave way and he fell to his knees in the gravel. When he scrambled up, he saw two hard hats approaching, their baked faces set in twin expressions of disbelief. One of them clamped Glen's shoulder. "Boy, there's people here. You could've damn killed somebody."

Glen shoved at the man's hand, but it came back like a steel spring. "Where's John Lowe?" he said.

"Hold on now."

Glen struggled, and the man's partner joined in. "Lowe!" Glen shouted. "John Lowe!"

"Keep still now. You've been told."

"I want to see him."

"Not till you calm down."

Glen fought until he knew he couldn't break loose. Gradually he let himself relax in their grasp, and when one of the men gave him a warning look and set off to summon Lowe, Glen counted to five and drove his fist into the other man's rib cage. A shocked grunt filled the air, and Glen sprinted for the trailer until a fist snagged him by the collar, jerking him down as if he were a child. Seconds later he was trying to shove a wide knee off his chest when he spotted John Lowe standing over him.

"Damn you," Glen hissed.

Lowe studied something in the distance. "What brought this on?"

"You sent her to Memphis."

Lowe shook his head and spat, the glob landing inches from Glen's ear. "All I know," he said, "is you're not fit to see her. Or raise my grandbaby."

The hard hat's knee pressed so hard Glen could barely raise his head. "She'll marry me," he gasped, his voice weak even in his own ears.

Lowe leaned down, the lines in his brow deepening. "You best forget that," he said.

An hour after dusk, Glen cut his lights and pulled onto the trailhead one mile from John Lowe's house. He parked between two cedars and hiked back to the highway, his father's .45 tucked into his belt. Only once did he see a vehicle, and when it neared he flattened himself in the ditch to wait, letting the bright beams wash past before he rose and went on. He kept to the grass when he reached Lowe's property, moving quietly beside the long drive until he could see porch columns splitting the darkness like streaks of moonlight. Staying near the ground, he crossed to the side yard where light from the study filled a wide window and revealed Lowe at his desk, back turned to the night.

Glen sank to his knees in the dampening grass. For several moments he studied Lowe's thick, hunched shoulders and iron-gray head. Tentatively, as if touching something foreign, he tapped the pistol. A quick pulse of power ran through him, and he pulled the gun from his belt. The .45's weight filled his hand, as real as a rock. He aimed a foot above Lowe's head. The report broke the night and Lowe whirled at his desk before ducking to the floor. Glen tightened both hands on the pistol and fired repeatedly, shattering what was left of the window and knocking down a painting on the far wall. When he realized the gun was empty he flung it toward the house, shouting, "She'll marry me. You hear?"

"You crazy bastard," Lowe shouted back. The voice was reedy and strained, but it hit Glen like a slap in the face. His head grew light and he began to move away, keeping to the shadows. By the time he reached the first bend in the drive he was sprinting.

Suddenly a shotgun blast ripped the limbs above his head, sending down a rain of leaves as he slid face-first in the gravel. The second blast bit into a trunk to his left and he scrambled behind the first large tree he could reach, hunkering there while Lowe cursed and raged from his porch. When the shouts finally ceased and Glen could hear no footsteps approaching, he gathered himself and sprinted again, racing toward the trailhead until his lungs burned inside his chest.

Once he reached the pickup he threw himself behind the wheel, swallowing great gulps of air as he slammed his fist on the dash. He imagined Lowe chambering rounds again, or perhaps screaming into a phone, demanding the sheriff hunt him down. The thought spread a coppery taste along his tongue and he stomped the accelerator, spinning his tires in the loose gravel until he gained the highway and pointed himself toward home. He drove fast, determined to see the place once more before fate fell on him like a net dropped from the sky.

When he turned into the driveway he half expected a squad of troopers to rush out of the shadows and drag him from his truck. Fighting paranoia, he drove close to the barn, grabbed his flashlight, and stepped out on weak legs.

The barn door's hinges creaked beneath his hand, and when he stepped through a faint odor of field dirt and sweat filled his memory. He stood for a moment, testing his eyes before flicking on the flashlight and roaming his gaze from one end of the structure to another. At the back, past the tack room with its ratty horse blankets and stiffened bridles, he made out the shapes of hay bales piled from floor to ceiling. The loft was also crowded with them—large, heavy bales he'd helped his father stack two summers ago in the swelter of June and July. His father's shape seemed nearly visible as Glen recalled a ropey forearm, then the curled power of grimed fingers as they gestured for another bale. He tried to clear the image from his mind, but reminders of his father were everywhere, from the workbench lining the east wall to the makeshift horse stalls the man had cobbled together after their mother ran off to California. The two Shetlands had been meant to salve lonely children's wounds, but the ponies foundered too often and were sold within a year.

Slowly Glen made his way to the twin stalls. A few patches of straw still lay hoof-trod in the pocked dirt. Kneeling, he gathered a handful and raised it to his face. The odor made him cough, but he remained there a long time, cracking the brittle straw in his fingers.

At dawn Glen heard a steady crunch of gravel on the drive below. He peered out the window beneath the eaves and watched three patrol cars roll slowly onto the property. When they eased to a stop, the passenger door of the middle vehicle came open and a tall, straight-backed old man whom Glen knew to be Sterle Hollis stepped out. Hollis passed his eyes over the house and barn, then let his gaze linger on Glen's truck. After a while he reached inside the patrol car and settled a pale feed cap on his head. "Don't a one of you go near that barn," he said, and started toward the house.

Glen settled back against a hay bale as Hollis approached the front door, loudly announcing himself as the Bond County sheriff. The words broke the morning quiet like pops from a cap gun, closer and sharper than Glen expected. For a moment he hunched between two bales, but when the sheriff boomed a warning through a bull horn, Glen stepped to the window and let Hollis and the deputies see him.

Hollis handed off the horn and moved beneath the window, his eyes tracing Glen's body, fixing on his hands. Glen raised empty palms and Hollis's posture slackened, his voice taking a softer tone. "All right, Son. I need you to stand right there. Jay Dee's coming up for you."

Glen's chest felt light, hollow. "Wait," he called. "I'll come down myself." Moving to a corner of the loft, he fumbled a match book from his pocket and lit two matches while Hollis started shouting again. Glen made sure the matches found a bed of straw before he descended the ladder. When he opened the barn door, two deputies took him down hard, smashing his face into the ground and wrenching his arms behind his back. Then he felt the cuffs encircle his wrists.

Moments later the deputies hauled him to his feet, pawing at him, pinching at his pockets. Finally Hollis himself took Glen by the elbow and guided him into the back seat of a patrol car. The door slammed and Glen was alone, window glass muffling the voices outside. He tested the cuffs once, knowing there would be no give to them as he rested his eyes on the field of yellowed alfalfa south of the barn. There had been rain last summer, rare through late June and July. The field could have yielded two cuttings at least, but with his father gone he hadn't even tried.

Glen focused his eyes on the barn roof and held his gaze steady even as the deputies slid into the front seat, the one on the passenger's side leaning back, snapping his fingers in front of Glen's face. "How're them cuffs? They too tight?" Glen ignored him, though from the corner of his vision he saw the driver shake his head and turn the key. The engine hummed quietly as the cruiser rolled nearer the barn and began a slow turn toward the highway. Twisting his shoulders to look through the back window, Glen took a sudden breath that hurt all the way to his sternum. Above the barn the sky had reddened, growing brighter with the rising sun.

# The End of Easy Breathing

From the porch glider, James Gann watched his daughter spray gravel as she barreled up the drive in her new Ford. He figured that at the pace she was traveling, she already knew what had happened in town that morning, but he told himself it couldn't be helped. She would have heard sooner or later, and it looked to be sooner. Rising stiffly, he peeked through the picture window to make sure Lila, his wife, was still in the living room, then hurried down the steps and met Jodi as she slammed the door of the truck.

"You'll wear the new off that way," he told her.

Her peach face always held a red tint, but now her cheeks were florid. "Why didn't you call me? I had to hear about it at work."

James tapped a knuckle on the pickup's white hood. "No use you getting upset. She's fine now."

"Fine! Daddy, she got lost on the square. If you can't watch her better than that, I'm going to the lawyer."

He swatted at a mosquito, a bite already burning his forearm. "I wish you'd hush about that. I'm tired of hearing it."

"I'm tired too. I'm sick with worry." Jodi pushed past him onto the porch, but on the top step she turned to glare down at him. "Were you drinking?"

"Don't start."

"You were!"

"Not even a beer, Missy."

"Then what happened?"

James smoothed his mustache with the back of his thumb, debating how much he wanted to say. His daughter's unblinking eyes demanded an answer. "Your mama had a spell in the bank lobby. I thought she'd be all right while I saw John Callahan, but she ran off."

Jodi slapped both hands against her thighs. "Why can't you keep your mind on her? You act like she don't mean a thing."

The accusation stung, and James stepped close to the porch. "You weren't there. You don't talk if you weren't there."

"I don't talk? About Mama? I wish you'd listen to yourself." She whirled and swept into the house, the screen door clattering behind her.

James took a deep breath and let it out slowly, trying to stay calm. The porch paint had begun to flake, and he toed the bottom step while a long, hard wish for civility went through him. He couldn't pretend he'd ever been close to Jodi, but now, with Lila so sick, he would welcome a truce. Turning to scan the yard, he let his eyes linger on the rope swing. Jodi had been six, maybe seven the day he hung it for her, and he remembered looking down from the ladder to see her peering through the oak limbs, faint green buds hovering above her head like a waiting garland. A rope or two had rotted since then, but he liked to keep a swing in that tree.

At the bottom of the near pasture the roan mare whinnied, and a moment later an answer came from the

Cochran place on the ridge. Normally James enjoyed any sound a horse could make, but today it rubbed him wrong. He went inside and took an elaborate amount of time checking the soles of his boots before he stepped into the living room. There Lila sat posed in the precise middle of the couch, her hands folded on her lap while Jodi tried to smooth the collar of her blouse.

James eased himself into the wing chair and waited, wishing for words that could bridge the silence. When the quiet went on too long, he said what he had wanted to say outside. "You can see she's fine. She don't like a fuss."

Jodi sighed loudly, and James pictured a kettle releasing steam. "Mama," Jodi said, "you feel better now that I'm here, don't you?"

James leaned forward and tried to catch Lila's gaze, but she didn't break her stare.

"Mama," Jodi said. "Answer me."

Finally Lila turned her head slightly. "Jodi Marie," she said. To James, the words seemed half sung, like someone cautiously searching for a new chord, but they were the first he had heard since early morning when she turned to him at breakfast and halted in mid-sentence. Her whole face had quivered, her lips elastic in the effort to find and shape his name. When she couldn't, she clutched her blouse close to her throat as if fending against a cold wind, and James watched while something faded behind her pupils.

Normally he wouldn't take her out of the house in that condition. The doctor had told him the spells must simply run their course, no way to break their hold or predict their duration. And he knew better than to trust Lila's pliancy, especially when she seemed content to move from room to room and let him remind her of favorite plants, perhaps the names of family members in recent photos. Too often some deep current of restlessness was at work in her, and she would wait for the moment when he became weary or inattentive. Then she would flee.

This morning, though, after she forgot his name, he felt like fleeing too. She had gone with him willingly, first for a ride around the farm, a soft, slow breeze flowing through the open windows of the truck cab, and then, when he remembered he needed to talk to Callahan about the mortgage, on to the bank in Lotten. For some reason the lobby itself had assured him. The orderly lines at the tellers' stations, the balanced arrangement of furniture in the seating area, even the neatness of the receptionist's desk had let him believe he could leave Lila for a moment or two without having to worry.

John Callahan never seemed to worry about anything. He was a big, glad-handing Oklahoman who had moved one state east because, as he liked to tell it, all the best trout were in Arkansas. James could breathe easy around him, even if all their conversations concluded on the subject of money, but this morning Callahan had barely begun to recount his weekend on the Spring River when the receptionist rapped twice and hurried through the door. James registered only her strained "Mr. Gann, your wife!" before rushing back to the lobby.

The couch where he left her was empty, but a small crowd of people had gathered at the glass doors opening onto the square. He shouldered through until he found himself outside on the sidewalk, staring at an accident. A pickup had crunched the back bumper of a Taurus, stalling traffic on the square. One of the drivers cursed and pointed toward the courthouse, where James spotted Lila crouching beneath a maple that shaded the lawn. By the time he reached her, he'd learned from the owner of the Taurus that she had run out into traffic and panicked, somehow losing her way in the forty yards of pavement that separated the bank from the courthouse lawn.

He knelt beside her, trying to still her trembling hands in his own.

Now, though, as Jodi stroked her hair, patted her back and shoulders, Lila seemed to be recouping small bits of herself. When she finally looked at him and smiled, James felt a knot of tension dissolving at the back of his neck. "Welcome home," he said.

A sudden worry entered her eyes. "My four-o'clocks. They need watering."

She hadn't planted four-o'clocks this year, but James told her the flowers would get water. There seemed no harm in the assurance, since in her mind it was a promise already kept. His word made it so. "Just count on me," he told her.

Jodi rose so quickly a couch spring groaned, and James saw that her face was fierce.

"What?" he said.

"I want to talk to you."

"Then talk."

She jerked her head toward the hall.

James growled beneath his breath and turned back to Lila, but her eyes had already locked in a stare, a tunnel whose distance he couldn't measure. He pinched the bridge of his nose and tried to ignore Jodi's heels on the hardwood, until her voice boomed from the hall. "Daddy!"

Hurriedly he patted Lila on the shoulder, then reached for the remote and tried to direct her attention to the television set. The antenna drew only two or three stations out of Jonesboro, each featuring a soap opera, but he couldn't tell that it mattered. He left the remote near Lila's knee and stepped into the hall.

Jodi met him with a loud whisper. "You've got gall, saying she can count on you."

He shrugged off what he thought was coming. "I did the best I could. She was gone before I knew it."

"I don't mean this morning. I mean that woman up on Summit Street."

The words hit him like a punch in the face. From what seemed a far distance, he could hear the television in the living room—two voices raised, a man and a woman. Before him, Jodi stood nodding, defiant as a teenager. "That's right," she said. "I know."

He wanted to put a hand over her mouth, mash her lips with his palm. "What do you think you know?"

"Lotten's not that big. People talk."

"And you listen, don't you?"

"When it touches Mama."

If he were outside he could kick a grain bucket, put a fist into a bale of hay. "I've not done a thing to hurt her."

"You don't think this hurts her? Just because she can't know?"

"I'm saying I don't mean it to."

"If you do it, you mean it," she said, and stepped around him as if he had no more feelings than a fence post. She strode into the living room and took Lila's face in her hands. "From now on, I'm gonna check on you every morning, every evening," she said. She waited a moment to see if Lila understood, then pressed a kiss to the blank forehead. On her way out, James tried to catch her and say something amenable, but she left so quickly the screen door leapt on its hinges.

Three hours later James watched Lila pace like a sentry at the picture window. She had latched onto the notion that Jodi would return before dark, and it was useless to tell her otherwise. A few minutes ago he'd had to call Jodi and endure the tension at the other end of the line while he explained that Lila wouldn't sit down, wouldn't eat or do anything else, until she came back. "It's that stuff you told her. She's got her times all confused," he'd said.

Now he sat in the worn wingback and studied the bottom of Lila's dress where the hem had come undone. A thin, fraying trail of paisley cloth dangled at her calf, and he waited for her to notice the loose hem as it brushed against her skin. In his mind's eye, he could see how the old Lila would react, the hard half-pout of her lips, the darkening displeasure of her eyes, until she looked up to find his face. "I'm a mess," she'd say, and she'd hurry down the hall to change. A moment later she'd return, the old dress draped over her arm as she entered the dining room and spread the garment on the table for mending.

James twisted around the wing of his chair and stared at the dining table, its surface lit by the lowering sunglow of evening. He wanted to retain the vision of Lila sitting there, bent to her sewing, but it was no use. The image faded as quickly as it had formed.

When he turned back to the living room, Lila was gone. He hurried into the hall, and through the open doorway he caught a glimpse of her already near the drive. "Lila!" he yelled. She glanced over her shoulder as he rushed onto the porch, but he could tell from her eyes that she wouldn't stop. He was about to yell again when he missed a porch step and pitched face first into the yard. Stunned, he lay still until the pain dulled in his jaw and hands. When he could get to his knees, he spat out a bloody string of saliva and a few blades of grass.

By now Lila was approaching the highway. He started after her, fearful this time would be like last spring when she made it all the way to the swollen creek and lost her balance trying to cross. But he had reached her in time, his brain screaming *Hold her Hold her* as he plunged into the water and grabbed her with the full force of his fear. They went under, his arms pinning hers to her sides while his legs fought the current. He was nearly prone and she above him, so he spun her face down in the water. Driving his knee into the gravel bottom, he managed to lift her out of water into rain, his lips tasting the slickened hair and the gaunt pale cheek in the instant before his chest began to heave.

That had been the other time, the end of easy breathing but not the end of breath itself. He'd made sure of it. Intending the same now, he forced himself to trot and caught her just as Jodi pulled in off the highway. He reached for Lila's wrist and she let him take it, passive as a chastened child, until Jodi stepped down from the cab. Then Lila pulled away.

Jodi took in the situation without a word. She opened the passenger side door and let Lila study the cab, then put a hand on her mother's back and stood close, coaxing her onto the running board, finally the seat itself. When Lila was settled, Jodi shut the door and gave him a hard stare. "Daddy, there's no way you can think this is working."

James yanked off his cap. "We'd have had a nice night if you hadn't confused her."

"Who confused her at the bank this morning? Or church last week?"

Exasperated, he dug at his scalp, then he slapped the cap back on his head. "I wish you'd stop all this."

"What would happen if I did?" She was about to turn away when something caught her eye. She leaned close, craning her neck to peer at his face. "Lord, is that grass you've got on your lip?"

James raked at his mustache. A single blade fluttered down and landed on the toe of his boot. He stared at it, too embarrassed to look up. "Will you watch her?"

Jodi started toward the pickup. "I'll take her home with me."

"No you won't. I mean watch her here, for a couple of hours."

Jodi stopped, hands on hips. "Jimmy's in summer school. He won't do a lick of homework if I'm not there."

"Have Dale watch him."

She made a face that said he should know better. "Daddy, I'm trying to help, but you can't have everything your way."

James rammed his hands into his front pockets and wondered if he should offer to pay her, then thought better of it. "I just want to know she'll be here when I get back."

"Back from where?"

"I need to go for a ride. Get some fresh air."

Jodi lowered her voice. "I know about your rides."

James swallowed. He could hear the dryness in his throat. "I didn't raise you to think that way."

"I've learned how lately."

He hunched his shoulders and let them sag, a gesture waiting for words. Finally he repeated himself. "I want to know she'll be here."

Jodi's face didn't change, but she nodded and motioned for him to get in the truck. He refused and started back on foot, letting his mind fill with the sound his boots made in the gravel. Slowly that sound was swallowed by the greater noise of the pickup grinding past. Glancing to his left, he saw Lila framed in the passenger side window, her gaze glassy and still.

Half an hour later James drove to the top of Summit Avenue, slowing as he passed Hannah McCrae's house to make sure her car was on the carport. He followed the long bend around the hill, past five or six clapboard houses just like hers, then turned onto Bennett and parked behind her house, where he saw the light in the kitchen. He passed through the rusty little back gate and knocked at the door.

When it opened, the sight of Hannah was like a thirst. She wore a tank top over faded jeans, and her sun-browned feet were bare. He could smell her perfume. "Can I come in?"

Hannah shook her head as if she'd heard a poor joke. "It's Sorry himself."

He wanted to reach for her, but he held back. "I know it's been awhile."

"Months, James. I stopped counting."

A splinter, barely visible, had split from the door jamb. He pulled it out. "It's not been where I can leave her."

"Then pick up a phone and say why. I deserve that much."

He nodded to say she did.

Hannah stepped back as if she meant to shut the door. "Tell me what's so special about tonight."

James had to search for an answer. Finally he said, "Jodi's there."

"And your first thought was to Tomcat it over here."

"It ain't like that."

"No, it's never like that." She swiped hard at her tinted bangs. "I could strangle you, James. I wish you'd go back home."

"I will. I just want a little time with you." At that she closed her eyes, and he thought the straight line of her mouth, maybe even her whole face, softened a little. "You smell good," he said. "I always liked the way you smelled."

She hid a laugh behind her hand, then reached out and touched a button on his shirt. "Liking's fine, James. It makes the memories sweet."

"Could be sweeter."

"No. We're past all that."

Something spoiled inside him. "You're not gonna let me in?" When she didn't answer, he leaned forward until her hand flattened against his chest. He could feel the firmness of her will, the foregone fact of her decision. *This hand, an inch from my heart*, he thought, and backed away.

"It's the right thing, James. We're too old to sneak around feeling guilty all the time. I am, anyway."

He tried once more to take her hand, but she moved beyond his reach and shut the door. The lock turned, and moments later the light went out in the kitchen.

Her yard sloped into the dusk. At the gate, he paused to make sure the futile little latch was set, then got in the pickup and stared at the bedroom window, thinking she might glance out. After a while a light came on and she crossed the narrow frame, but she didn't turn her head. When the light died, he started the pickup and drove away.

Near the center of town, James circled the square and headed down Jefferson Avenue, where on weekends teenage cruisers lit the night like streams of fireflies. For now the street was his. He told himself he wasn't thirsty, that he wouldn't do anything more than look for a quick game of pool, or maybe drive by the baseball fields and catch an inning or two of Little League. But by the time he reached the Conoco station near the city limits, he'd already worked out a model of moderation—how two six packs would translate into a beer a night for twelve nights, and he didn't see how Jodi, or anyone else, could object to that.

After making the purchase, he drove out to the old railroad tracks south of town and parked near a stretch of pasture land where he'd hauled hay as a boy. He downed the first beer in one long quaff and told himself he was done, but his thirst had been roused and in a few minutes the floorboard was littered with empty cans, so many he knew it no longer mattered if he stopped. When there was nothing left to drink, he stumbled to the edge of the pasture and leaned against a fence post while he relieved himself. In the distance he could hear coyotes yipping into the night, and then a sudden, eerie silence. He shoved himself from the fence post and nearly lost his balance, the groan of old fence wire humming in his ears. He made it back to the pickup, and after fumbling for his keys, he started home. He was admiring the beautifully mottled moon that had descended to fill his windshield when a sheriff's deputy pulled him over.

At first the young man seemed friendly, but after he asked James to step out of the pickup, James couldn't make him understand that Lila was waiting for him, that she sometimes grew confused and ran off. He tried to get back in the pickup, saying Jodi would take Lila from him if he didn't return, but the young man wouldn't let him. Finally they struggled and James ended up on the ground, his breath coming short and fast and his face pressed into the weeds that grew along the shoulder of the road.

The next morning, James opened his eyes to the pale, peeling walls of a cell no larger than a clothes closet. His pillow reeked, and he knew in an instant where he was. He felt hot and groggy, as if a mean flu had settled in his body and stayed too long. After a while he sat up and squinted at the shaft of sunlight that came through the little block window on the east wall. It reminded him of something, and he recoiled. He couldn't escape the memory though, that bright afternoon nearly a decade ago when he decided, after too many beers, that it was time he took his grandson for a horseback ride. The boy was barely two, staying for the first time with his grandfather while Lila and Jodi went shopping in town, and somehow James spawned the notion to saddle the sorrel stallion and carry the boy in the crook of his arm as he cantered about the paddock. At some point Jimmy slipped his hold and ended up on the ground, laughter turning to sobs as James circled closer and closer, trying to lift the child into the saddle again. And then there was his daughter's sudden rush against the stallion's chest, the slaps and curses as she drove the horse away. Only then, as James reined about, did he see the blood that covered one side of Jimmy's face. Frozen, he watched Jodi scoop her son in her arms and race with Lila back to the car. They had already roared away, leaving a trail of dust the length of the drive, before he could move again. Dismounting, he stripped the stallion of bridle and saddle, leaving the tack where it fell. Driven by shame, he stumbled toward the barn and threw himself into the far stall, crouching on his heels in the sun-blocked darkness while he pounded his forehead with the back of his fists.

He had no idea how long he stayed there, but eventually a shaft of light flashed across the doorway and he heard slow steps coming toward the stall, steps he knew. When he looked up, Lila was kneeling at the door. There would be a scar, she told him, but no damage to the head. It might have been a rock, or a glancing blow, perhaps no kick at all.

He crawled to her, letting his head fall on her breast. He felt her grasp the back of his shirt and ball the cloth in her fists as if she meant to cling to him no matter what harm he had done, and after a while he rose with her and let her lead him from the barn.

Now he lay back on the cot and the stinking pillow, gripping himself tightly. He thought how long it had been since he'd felt her arms about him. Taking the pillow from behind his head, he placed it over his mouth so that he wouldn't hear himself plead for what couldn't be, that she might come to him and lead him once again into the glaring light of day.

Half an hour later, a graying, paunchy deputy opened the cell door and told James that if he could pass a breathalyzer, he'd be allowed to call a bail bondsman. James agreed to try, and when the deputy pronounced him sober, he started the process of regaining his freedom. He'd signed several papers, nodding dutifully anytime the bondsman's voice grew firm, when he heard Jodi in the lobby. He looked from the deputy to the bondsman, then back again. "Who called her?"

The deputy hitched his belt. "Benson might have, after he brought you in. He said they went to school together."

James's first instinct was to chuck it all, tell them he'd just as soon they lock him up again, but the thought of Lila changed his mind. He followed the men into the front alcove and met Jodi's eyes, bracing himself for a barrage. "You got me," he said. "I messed up."

Jodi took a slow breath. "Yes, Daddy. You did."

"I guess your mama's with you, at your place."

"That's best, don't you think?"

James felt for his keys, fishing for them in what turned out to be an empty front pocket. "I think they owe me some property."

"Dale's got your truck. They say I can drive you home."

Heat rose in his face. "You care anything about what I say?"

Jodi jerked her purse strap higher on her shoulder. "Don't talk to me about caring," she said.

Her eyes looked veiny and red. He tried to steel himself, so he wouldn't fold in front of her. "Why aren't you at work?"

"I took off."

"This is costing you money then?"

"If that's how you look at it."

He didn't like her losing wages. The garment factory couldn't be trusted for steady work, and she had the new truck to pay for. "I been trouble enough," he said.

She jerked the purse strap again and turned for the door. He followed her out to the parking lot, where late morning glare ricocheted from windshield to windshield. Squinting against the brightness, he stayed several steps behind until they reached her pickup.

"I want to see her," he said.

Jodi's shoulders straightened. "Daddy, just stay home for a day or two. It'll be easier that way."

"Easier for who?"

She unlocked the passenger door and slung it open. "You just said you're through causing trouble."

"I didn't think you'd grudge me this."

"Look where we're standing, Daddy! I didn't put you here."

She stalked around the front of the pickup and climbed behind the wheel. Staring straight ahead, she said, "Get in or walk. I don't care which."

James waited until she turned the key in the ignition before he climbed in. She accelerated so hard out of the parking lot that he expected a bumpy trip home. The ride surprised him, though, the new vehicle gliding through town and onto the highway with a comfortable sensation that made him think of treading soft carpet. The sun grew warm on his face, coaxing his eyes closed, and he thought how sleep could come as easily as breath. It could shut out last night, even Jodi and her endless demands. But then he remembered Lila, how only yesterday she had struggled to voice his name. Against a great weariness he opened his eyes, stared as straight at the sun as he could bear.

# FOR YOU

Joe Barnes held the razor away from his neck while he stared at the ten-year-old in the doorway. Her stringy yellow hair was matted to one cheek and she wore an old T-shirt that bottomed at her knees, but there were no signs of sleepiness in her face. She looked at him with the same hard frown her mother sometimes used when she thought he was too foolish to exist, and Joe decided he'd rather stare at his own face in the mirror. He stuck out his chin and ran the razor down his neck in one long stroke, but before he could rinse the blade he heard the girl's voice.

"Are you gonna do it?"

He looked at her again. The frown was so severe her eyelids were slits. She rested one hand on her hip, and her elbow grazed the doorframe.

"Do what?"

"You know what."

He turned back to the mirror and tried to remember what he looked like without the beard. "I'm thinking about it."

"Today?"

"Maybe."

"You ain't got enough lather. That's just for your neck."

He took another swipe with the razor, watching her out of the corner of his eye. "Let me worry about what's enough, okay?"

She crinkled her nose as if she smelled a bad odor. "I worry about what I want to."

"You've got some strange worries."

"You're strange all right."

It was a perfect exit line, a hit-and-run insult she knew he wouldn't counter, and he expected her to twist on her bare feet and leave. Instead, she stayed planted in the doorway. He could feel her watching as he brought the razor down over his Adam's apple and finished with three quick strokes where the whiskers grew in a swirl at the bottom of his neck. He stored the razor in the medicine cabinet and cupped his hands beneath the warming stream of water. By the time he splashed his neck the water was hot enough to sting, but the girl hadn't moved.

"You ever hear of privacy?"

She said nothing, her frown still severe. He stepped to the door and put his hand on the knob. "Scoot!" When she didn't move, he focused his eyes on the old mill print in the hallway and began to close the door. Her hand smacked against the wood and he felt her small, useless resistance. Then she took her hand away and the door slammed shut, the sound so loud it surprised him.

A moment later the shower seemed loud too, like rain on a tin roof. He stepped in and let the water break on the back of his neck. The water slid down his shoulders in separate streams and he tried to follow each stream with his mind, but his thoughts kept returning to the girl. She was full of odd requests. For a month after he and Ellen were married, she'd begged him to take her to the horse races at Hot Springs, but she'd lost interest the moment he agreed. Or once she'd asked him not to speak to her at Blue Hill, her grade school where he was head janitor. The next day he'd seen her and a classmate in the hall and she'd sung out, "Hi, Joe," when he passed by. Now, for a week almost, she'd been after him to shave his beard. He couldn't make sense of it, and he doubted she could either.

By the time he made it to the kitchen he was late for breakfast. Ellen had eggs on the stove for him, but her plate was already in the sink and she was finishing her coffee at the table. He poured a cup for himself and stared at the random pile of wood in the back yard. The Spencer boy had brought a load last Saturday, tossing small, uneven logs off the back of his truck and letting them land near the fence, where they had lain for a week. Joe decided he ought to work them up today. He ought to change the oil in Ellen's Focus too.

Ellen sat with her back turned to him, huddled in the green terrycloth robe he'd given her a year ago Christmas. He'd wanted her to have something softer against her skin than his hands could be. She'd liked it so much she had him get a smaller one for Jenny, but the girl preferred those huge T-shirts that hung to her knees.

Joe sipped the weak coffee and grimaced. "I guess she's mad at me," he said.

Ellen turned, cradling the cup in her lap as if it gave warmth. "She said you shut the door on her."

"I had to shower."

"She said you pushed her."

He waited. In a moment he said, "She wouldn't get out."

Ellen turned away, and Joe thought of the first time he'd seen her. She was fixing a flat at the crossroads north of the school, and by the time he'd U-turned and made his way back to the Focus, she had the lugs off and was about to pull the tire. The look she gave him when he stepped out of his truck made him want to get back in and drive away fast.

"She's just blowing things up again," he said. "She wasn't hurt."

Ellen hooked a fistful of hair behind her ear and shook her head. "You're too rough with her. You don't know how to talk to her."

He splattered the sink with what was left of his coffee. That morning when Ellen turned to him with the lug wrench in her hand, he asked if she needed help and she dismissed him the way she'd tell a waitress she didn't want her drink refilled. Then the little girl appeared from somewhere on the other side of the car and stood near her mother. "Hey," he said, raising his hand as if taking an oath. She merely stared, her blue eyes so steady he thought she might be studying his soul for judgment. He'd had no idea what her verdict would be.

He ran the faucet full blast to rinse the sink and watched the water trickle down the drain. "She catches me off guard. Those things she asks."

"You puzzle her too. She needs you to be patient."

"How long? She's been in this house two years."

Ellen shrugged. "A while longer, I guess."

The words stopped him, made him think of roads he didn't want to travel. "You know I love you."

Ellen pushed the cup deeper into her lap. "Yes," she said.

Joe had been at the woodpile for the better part of an hour when he noticed the girl watching him, spying on him almost. She was trying to stay behind the riding lawn mower at the far end of the carport, but that flash of yellow hair was the brightest thing in the winter-gray landscape. He tried to ignore her, but when he lifted the axe above his head he caught a spot of gold on the corner of his eye and it remained there, gilding the edge of his vision as he sank the axe blade into the wood. The last block of oak split cleanly and he tossed the axe on the ground, then gathered a small armload of wood and dumped it into the wheelbarrow. As he trundled the wood toward the fence, his breath formed pale white plumes in the air.

"You'll get cold just standing around," he called back to her. "Why don't you help me get this wood up?"

The last thing he expected was for her to help him. She'd built a creed out of being contrary, and the quickest way to get rid of her would be to invite her along. He reached the waist-high stack of wood near the fence and began to even out the top row, tossing a few sticks here and there to fill in the gaps. When he was ready to start a new row he turned back to the wheelbarrow and saw her standing beside it. She was picking at a patch of rust with her bare hands.

"Don't you have any gloves?"

She made a face as if she'd been insulted. "Are you gonna stack all that wood today?"

"I plan to."

"It's a lot of wood," she said, running her hand back and forth along the side of the wheelbarrow as if she held a piece of sandpaper. When she lifted the hand, rust had reddened her palm. She raised it toward his face like a prize.

"You need gloves," he said again.

She wiped her hand on the bottom of her coat and started back to the house. Watching her, he wondered what he would have to do to make her smile. Then a sudden gust raked his face and neck and he shouted, "Bye." She walked on—steady, mincing little steps that caused her head to bob—and he studied her back until she disappeared inside the house.

By the time he had all the wood stacked against the fence, he could feel his feet growing cold inside his boots. He pushed the wheelbarrow around the side of the house and opened the little vinyl building that served as his tool shed. There he squeezed the wheelbarrow into an open space between two paint-stained sawhorses and headed back to the house.

When he stepped in out of the cold, the warmth of the kitchen was like a balm. He could smell beans on the stove and cornbread in the oven, and Ellen stood by the sink peeling onions. He took a step toward her, but she pointed the knife at his feet before he could move off the mat. "Check your boots," she said. "I don't want you tracking in mud."

He pulled off his boots and padded heavily across the room. The smell of the food and the memory of wood stacked neatly along the fence gave him a quick feeling of prosperity. He reached for a thin slice of onion as Ellen rinsed the knife beneath the faucet. "It's a cold one," he said.

"I'm glad you got the wood up. It makes the yard look neater."

He nodded and took a bite of the onion. It was juicy and sweet, and his mouth didn't begin to burn until after he'd swallowed. Quickly he ate the rest of the slice and ran himself a glass of water. "Tried to get Jenny to help me," he said.

"I saw." She studied the long line of wood outside the window. He let his eyes roam beyond the fence to the thin stand of scrub oak atop the near ridge. The hard, bare limbs made him think of hawks' talons.

"I'm about to give up," he said. "I don't know what she wants from me."

"What did she ask for?"

"When?"

"This morning."

"What she's not gonna get."

He turned from the window expecting to see her frown, but instead he noticed her eyes. They looked as if they had seen a new and pleasing thing. "Tell me," she said.

◆   ◆   ◆

He knew he was looking at his own face in the mirror, the same thick round cheeks and puffy chin that had always been there beneath the beard, but now the skin looked pale and sickly, like that of a man who'd been shut away from sunlight. He'd never been handsome, never even worried about trimming the beard on a regular basis, but now he found himself staring at someone he didn't know and didn't particularly want to be. He couldn't imagine why he'd gone to the trouble. Suddenly Ellen's voice came muffled through the wood. "Hurry up. We're waiting."

Running a comb through his hair, he realized his wife had never seen him without the beard. He shook his head at the strange twin trapped in the mirror and turned his back on him.

Ellen was waiting in the living room, and he saw her lips part in a faint smile. The girl sat at one end of the couch with a book in her lap. She hadn't even looked up.

"Jen," Ellen called.

Slowly the girl closed the book and looked at her mother, then at Joe. Her expression didn't change, and he wondered if she recognized him. He could feel his face tingling, the skin raw and warm. He went to the couch and sat down beside her. "I did it," he said. When her expression still didn't change, he added, "For you."

She scanned his face, searching for some point of interest. Then her eyes stilled and she raised one small hand to his cheek. For a moment he felt warmth against his skin. Then she shifted her eyes and stared at her hand, at the thin red smear on her fingertips. When she looked at him again, she was smiling.

Backlit by the moon, the oaks on the east ridge loomed black in the blue night. Joe studied them from the bedroom window, his forearms crossed on the sill. The trees seemed blacker by night, their dark limbs curled like claws beneath the pearly moon. Raising one hand in a loose fist, he let it rest against the glass.

She scarcely made a sound when she entered, only a soft footfall in the doorway and the sweep of her hand on the light switch. Then the room glowed behind him and he saw not trees on the ridge but his shorn face in the window. Turning, he watched surprise register in her eyes. "Just me," he said quickly.

A dimple deepened in her cheek, like a raindrop on still water. She opened the bureau and took out her nightgown. "I'd know you anywhere."

He watched the way she disrobed, stepping out of her clothes more casually than he could shed a pair of coveralls and dropping her jeans and top on the rounded arm of the rocker. When she slipped her nightgown over her head, he thought of a woman rising out of deep water, pale arms splitting the surface of an invisible sea. Her hands dropped to her sides and suddenly she stared at him from across the room, her eyes locked hard on his face. "That was nice what you did," she said. "I didn't think you would."

He cut his eyes to the doorway. "You asked me."

"Jen asked you."

"It's the same thing."

"No. It's not."

The bed was between them, the plain gray comforter grown pale, almost white, with use. He sat down on the edge of the bed and pulled off his boots, then spoke to her over his shoulder. "You're seeing something that ain't there."

He waited for her voice, listened for it amid the creaking of the bedsprings as he leaned forward and set the boots in the corner. In a moment he felt her weight on the bed as she moved toward him. She slipped a hand inside his collar and softly stroked the back of his neck. "I know what I see," she said, then lifted her hand from his neck and began to trace his jaw with her fingers. He didn't want her to touch his face, so he took her hand and held it near his thigh. After a while she pulled her hand free and placed it atop his, lacing their fingers. "Adopt her," she said.

He wanted to say her name, but he couldn't.

"It's all I ask," she said.

"It's too much."

She took her hand away. Briefly she sat there, leaning lightly against him, then got up and turned back the cover on her side of the bed.

He waited until she had settled herself, then rose and took off his clothes and dropped them at the edge of the bureau. He hit the light switch to darken the room, and on his way back to the bed he glanced out the window, where the oaks loomed black and tangled beyond the glass.

He didn't shave on Sunday, and by Monday morning his jaws were lightly shadowed by grizzle. At Blue Hill the students he passed in the halls peered at his face as if they were spying something forbidden, and so did a few of the teachers. Only once did he catch sight of Jenny. Her class came streaming down the hall toward the gym, and she passed by him as if he were a stranger.

Toward noon he made a quick round with his dust mop and finished as the first of the lunch bells rang. A class of first graders spilled loosely into the hall and he made his way past them so that he could duck into the small storage room beneath the stage. The room was windowless, with close, shelf-lined walls, and at his feet were boxes of copy paper and toner that occupied most of the floor space. His desk was there though, an old metal one discarded by the principal, and he sat down and wolfed the two ham sandwiches and the can of Coke he'd packed that morning. When he finished he pulled on his coat and went outside.

The air was still. In the distance he could hear the younger children already playing on the far side of the building. He listened for a while and realized he couldn't tell anything from the sounds, couldn't separate a squeal of laughter from one of pain or complaint. All the voices seemed high pitched and distant, their rhythms teasing his tongue like a language he'd once known but could no longer remember.

Eventually he tired of listening. He had another quarter hour before he was due inside, so he left the parking lot and headed toward the field at the south end of the school grounds. There was a small pond at the edge of the field and he'd stretched a fence around its banks years ago. He kept telling the principal the pond ought to be filled with dirt, just to be sure no kid drowned there, but so far his fence was the only safeguard.

The pond looked low. Field grass rose high and sere about its banks. He leaned against a fence post and felt it give an inch or two beneath his weight. The sun was only a faint hint of gold overhead, and he couldn't find its reflection in the dull gray eye of the water. *Why do they want to come here,* he thought. *Why are they drawn to such a ragged place?* He reached for the top of a fence post, testing the resolve of cedar. An odor rose, and suddenly he remembered the thick, choking taste of chlorine and the terror invading his limbs as he tried to call for his father. Sinking, he thought of his voice as a rope thrown above the water, a short, thin rope aimed at his father's back where his father stood talking with a woman at the edge of the hotel pool, but the rope did not reach. He went down, his mind filling with the image of his father's back, fixed and still as a distant wall. Then he felt a hand about his wrist and someone pulled him to the surface. He remembered faces in a circle around him, faces holding more curiosity than fear, and finally his father burst into the circle and grabbed him by the shoulders. He could remember the shaking, the loud hard voice that called him a fool, and suddenly his hands found the fence post and he threw his weight against its resistance. The post snapped just above the ground and he heard the quick moan of the wire as the fence snagged. He cursed, quietly and out of old despair, then started back toward the school.

The school buses rolled out of the parking lot at three. Clifford Toms, the skinny night man, was late, and Joe spent an extra thirty minutes sweeping out classrooms before Toms showed up with a tired excuse about having to take his mother-in-law to the doctor. When Joe arrived home, he found Ellen and the girl arguing in the kitchen because the girl hadn't done the dishes from the night before. One look at their taut faces told him he didn't want any part of it. "I need a shower," he grumbled.

In the bathroom he turned the shower faucet on full blast and tilted his head so the water would pound him in the face. He wanted the water to be louder, so loud he couldn't hear his own thoughts, but there was no such deafness.

When he stepped out of the shower, he heard the voices. The girl's was clearest, its pitch high and strained, but Ellen's was strong too. Suddenly the yelling stopped and the back door slammed. He threw on his clothes and bumped into Ellen in the hall, her right hand covered in a towel. He could see blood seeping through the cloth. "What did she do to you?" he yelled.

Ellen stared at him for a moment before anger flashed in her eyes. "She didn't do anything. I forgot the knife was in the sink."

Joe tried to check her hand, but she brushed him away and hurried to her daughter's room. She grabbed a coat off the bed, but he stopped her at the doorway. "Let me see it," he demanded.

"She's out there without her coat."

"She'll come in when she gets cold."

Ellen tried to push past him, but he wouldn't let her. "You're not going outside," he said. "I'll take her the coat." She pushed again, but he didn't move. "I said I'll take it."

Finally she shoved the coat at his chest and whirled away from him, settling herself on her daughter's bed. "Bring her back in," she said.

Shaking his head, he turned down the hallway and went outside, breasting the wind in a shirt that lay damp against his skin. He made his way across the backyard and was about to circle the house when he caught a flash of yellow hair high on the ridge, among the oaks. He stared for a moment, and the wind that came slashing down the hill felt as if it would cut him in two. He raised the small coat to his chest and moved forward, through the gate and on into the pasture. Tiny bits of snow whipped in the air, and he broke into a lumbering run.

By the time he neared the trees he was short of breath. He stopped and studied the thin woods, finally spotting her crouched behind one of the oaks, her head ducked nearly to her knees. He started toward her. "Jenny," he called, and saw her head rise. As he came nearer she stood and held out her hand for the coat. He tried to slip it over her shoulders but she twisted away, grabbing it from him as she turned and started farther up the ridge.

Anger surged within him. He leaped and caught her by the collar, then jerked her into his lap as he sat back against a tree trunk. She was still for only a moment before turning on him, her small hands scratching at his eyes and her feet pounding his knees and shins. He wrapped her in his arms and tried to calm her with his strength, but she sank her teeth into his forearm. The pain was instant, a cold burning that spread through his whole left side. With his free hand he grabbed the back of her neck and closed his fist in a tangle of yellow hair, readying himself to pull back hard, to yank her loose from him and teach her a lesson in pain. But then he saw her open eye, its pale blue drop like a lake of sorrow. He could feel himself falling toward that eye, and he heard her low, growling moan on the cold air. Clenching his teeth against the pain, he leaned his head close to hers. "I can hear you," he said. "I can hear you."

# JUDGMENT CALL

N orman Kissee pressed the strike button on his umpire's indicator and settled in for the next pitch, which came in hot, hissing high and a bit inside before he could register the catcher's lack of movement. The ball caught him flush above the heart and rode up under his chin, knocking his mask askew as he staggered backward and toppled. He lay stunned for a moment, spread-eagled behind home plate before reaching up to shove the mask off his forehead. Above him faces gathered in a circle. He stared back, deciding he disliked being laid out like this, especially while everyone was watching. He struggled to a sitting position, slapping away the hands that reached out to him until one hand thumped him on the shoulder and he realized his partner, Burl Stewart, was kneeling beside him.

"Take it slow, Kiss. You got drilled big time."

Norman's chest felt as if he had run into the butt end of a corner post, but he replayed the pitch in his mind, watching the fast ball bore toward him with no catcher's mitt moving into view. Then he searched the faces above him. Both coaches were there, and so was the young pitcher, gawking over their shoulders and worrying he might have killed someone. Norman nodded to him. "Relax kid. You don't throw hard enough to break anything."

Burl helped him to his feet and Norman took a moment to steady his legs before looking for the catcher, Cody Frazier. The young man was standing near the on-deck circle, gazing into the sparse crowd as if he hoped to spot a pretty girl. Norman glared. There were words he wanted to say, words that surged against his clenched teeth and would have sounded something like *You're your daddy's boy all right* if he had let them escape, but he couldn't do that. Instead he swallowed gall exactly the way he had three weeks ago when he'd thrown Frazier out of a game down in Little Rock.

Norman had been behind the plate that day too. Cody began arguing balls and strikes in the bottom of the first when his pitcher walked the bases loaded and eventually gave up three runs. By the top of the fifth the score was 5-0, and when Norman called Cody out on a sinking fastball, the kid exploded. He hurled the bat toward the dugout and let loose a barrage of curses, so Norman tossed him instantly. If the third base coach hadn't wrapped Cody in a bear hug and hauled him away, the boy would have thrown punches, Norman was sure. He was less certain he'd have checked his own fists.

Now he moved toward the on-deck circle, thinking he at least had to confront the kid, make him say he'd been crossed up on the pitch even if that was untrue, but Burl stepped in front of him and stood brushing dust off the mask Norman had flung away. Burl seemed determined to get the mask perfectly clean. "No sense in round two," he mumbled, and when Norman tried to step around him Burl planted the mask in the middle of Norman's chest. "No sense," he said again. For five summers Burl had partnered with Norman, working American Legion games in order to escape the monotony of his insurance business while Norman added a few dollars to his teacher's salary. Norman took a deep breath and decided to trust Burl more than himself. "Let's play ball," he barked.

Moments later Cody returned and crouched behind home plate as if nothing had happened. Burl trotted out to his position beyond second base, only a few steps from the outfield grass. The pitcher, who still seemed wide-eyed and worried, fidgeted near the rubber until Norman shouted "Let's go." When the hitter stepped in and assumed a stance in imitation of Buster Posey, Norman felt for his chest protector and adjusted it inside his shirt.

Again the pitch was a fast ball, again high. The hitter bailed and for a moment Norman saw nothing between himself and the spinning seams. Then a glove appeared and the ball popped the pocket. "Whew," Cody sang out. "That one almost got away."

Norman gritted his teeth, fighting the urge to plant an iron-toed shoe in the kid's backside. "Ball two," he said.

The next pitch broke low, biting dirt in front of the plate and skipping between Cody's legs. Norman felt a brush of his pant leg as the ball went through to the back stop, then he took a hard bump as Cody spun and nearly flattened him going after the ball. "Nobody on base," Norman shouted.

Cody lifted his mask as he came back with the ball. "Just hustling," he said, a wide grin splitting his face. "Got to play the right way."

"That means knowing the game situation."

"We have a situation?" Cody asked, mock curiosity animating his face before he whistled the return throw past Norman's head. Norman judged the crack of the pitcher's glove the loudest he'd heard all game.

On the mound, the pitcher looked increasingly rattled. He shook off several signs before lobbing what looked like a cross between a change-up and an intentional ball four. In response his coach came hot-footing out of the dugout even before the hitter started to first. "Got some changes," he called, and Norman was grateful to hear one involved Cody replacing the right fielder, a big kid named Buckner, who trotted in to take the mound. Cody began removing the catcher's gear at home plate, and as he unbuckled his shin guards Norman caught the words just above the rustling of the crowd. "Sleep tight, Kissee. You'll be plenty sore tomorrow."

When the boy straightened, Norman fixed him with a stare, daring him to wink, to twitch even one corner of his mouth. Cody met Norman's stare, not moving until his back-up cautiously pulled the shin guard from his hand.

After the game, when the crowd had filed out and a crew from the Lotten Parks and Recreation Department began to pick up trash, Norman found a shaded spot near the top of the bleachers behind the visitors' dugout. A mini-grove of five tall cedars cast him in soft shadow, and although he wanted to be alone, he didn't object when Burl sat down and handed him a lukewarm can of diet Coke.

Studying the empty field, Burl pushed out his belly and began to rub his lower back. "Don't know about you, but anymore I like it best like this, when all the sweat and struggle is done." A moment later he laughed. "I sound like an old man."

"We're getting there, both of us."

"But I have a decade head start."

Norman nodded and popped the Coke can, curious to see how Burl would bring up Cody Frazier. A late afternoon breeze cooled him through the dampness of his shirt.

Burl lifted his collar, jiggling the cloth to make the most of the breeze. "That catcher we've got. Like a dog with a bone, ain't he?"

Norman decided he respected the direct approach. It was probably what he would try with one of his students. "I should have told you," he said. "It's more than a beef about a call."

"I had a notion. We carried the policy on his daddy, you know."

Norman stared into the high school parking lot beyond right field. "No, I didn't."

"Pure accident. That beer cooler shrunk the settlement though."

Norman found that if he shut his eyes, the sun still shone brightly enough to glare. "It doesn't keep me up at night," he said.

"No reason it should. It was his boat, and him at the wheel." Burl took a long drink, draining the can and crushing the middle until it took on an hourglass shape. "But I can see how it might bother a boy the age this one's getting to be. Make him brood on things nobody can answer."

Norman felt a flutter of sickness in his stomach. In a moment the flutter transformed, tightening into a familiar knot he always pictured as a child's fist. "We had a round or two before he transferred," he said. "He ought to have a year left out there at Arditi."

"Not a bad little school. They have a kid playing for the Razorbacks right now."

"I know. If he's good enough for a scholarship he'll get one."

"I imagine so," Burl said. He stood up, surveying the field. Then he looked down at Norman. "Unless that temper wrecks him."

From the top of the stands, Norman watched Burl's Lexus pull out of the parking lot and cross the railroad tracks, heading south toward his comfortable red brick home in the Lake Haven subdivision. Norman figured he ought to head home himself, but the game had been quick despite the interruption, and he decided a short walk might help him work out some of the soreness in his chest. Behind the stands lay a small complex of Little League fields, and Norman made his way to the farthest one. There a team of third or fourth graders was taking fielding practice, the coach slapping ground balls around the infield and occasionally lifting soft flies to the outfield.

As Norman took a place at the edge of the bleachers, one of several mothers lifted her head from a cell phone and noticed his uniform. "Hey, Ump," she called, "I don't think they're ready for prime time."

Norman grunted and settled in to watch, letting a bit of tension drain away as he studied the tiny players, some earnest in their attempts to learn the game, others merely passing time. When the shortstop let a ground ball roll between stubby, tanned legs, Norman looked back to the woman with the cell phone. She cocked an eyebrow and sighed. "See what I mean?"

"I do."

Eventually Norman lost interest and scanned the bleachers, noticing a general absence of fathers. He glanced at his watch, which read a little after 4:00. Nancy would expect him soon, and he grimaced at the thought that someone who saw the game might call to check on him. His wife was a worrier, and although he didn't relish telling her about the incident, he knew she would have even more questions if she heard the news from someone else.

Driving the winding road to his place outside town, Norman mulled over how much he should say, recalling that on the night he threw Cody out of the Little Rock game he had eaten dinner with Nancy and the girls without mentioning the ejection. His two daughters would have been excited merely by the idea of their father as the center of a spectacle, all the yelling and cursing an added bonus. Nancy would have been quieter though, her questions more probing. After the meal they'd all watched a mindless talent competition on television, and Norman waited until everyone else had gone to bed before sitting down to fill out the American Legion Ejection Report. It was a standard form he'd completed a couple of times in the past, not a high number considering he'd been calling games for more than a decade. But this time the term "ejected person" stopped him. It should have been a simple enough task to write the name Cody Frazier, yet he couldn't help feeling he'd be stamping the kid with some kind of permanent label. Besides, the next line asked him to describe any "unusual circumstances." All he had to do was mention the thrown bat, but that alone would have felt like a half truth. He'd stewed for nearly thirty minutes, not knowing how to fill the white space without including the afternoon fifteen years ago when Cody's father had talked him into going fishing.

Norman had played ball with Gene Frazier in high school, but they'd gone separate ways since graduation, so Norman was surprised when Gene called him up and insisted they try for bass at Catamount Bay. At first Norman made excuses, saying he didn't fish much, that he was newly married and needed to work on the little two-bedroom he and Nancy had just purchased. But Gene made a vague offer of future help, so Norman decided removing multiple layers of vinyl from the kitchen floor could wait a day or two. He met Gene at an old dock at the lower end of the lake, and after a couple of beers they were on the water looking for a likely spot free of boaters and fellow fishermen.

At first they said little to each other, the silence reminding Norman that aside from baseball they had never spent much time together. Finally Gene forced a laugh. "I can't believe you're teaching," he said as he slowed the boat and turned back toward the shoreline, intent on finding good brush. "I mean, don't you get tired of school? There's a whole world out here."

Norman took in the wide water, the great limestone bluffs that always nudged his imagination and made him think of the Osage and their long ago lives. "I guess so," he said.

Gene shook his head. "You get summers off though. That's the sweet deal of it."

"There's work to do when we're not in class."

"Sure," Gene said, scrunching his face in an exaggerated wink that made Norman wonder how many beers he'd already downed. "Wish I had a racket like that."

Norman thought back to Gene the athlete, a tough, wiry third basemen with a good throwing arm and a knack for needling opposing teams. He'd filled out in the last decade, so much so Norman noticed soft flesh stretching the faded knit shirt, a company issued polo with an ArkMo logo on the left chest pocket. Gene wore it tucked into a frayed pair of blue jeans, a roll of beer belly spilling over the waistband.

"How's it going over at the plant?" Norman asked, pointing to the logo. "I hear they have good benefits."

Gene guided the boat toward the mouth of Sandfort Cove. "Used to, but I wouldn't know now. Hand me something from the cooler, okay."

Norman noticed Gene's face harden and sensed a change, sudden and unpredictable. Like weather on a lake, he thought, and lifted the lid of the cooler. Only beer nestled in the ice.

"They do water patrols out here, don't they?"

"School's out, Teach."

Norman scanned the cove. He could spot only one or two boats in the distance. Over the side, the water looked murkier than he expected for an Ozark lake, and he couldn't guess the depth. He handed Gene a Coors. "You're well stocked."

"Just being a good host," Gene said, and popped the top with a forefinger. "No worries."

Norman considered how much work was left in order to renovate his house, how much the planned additions would take from his future paychecks. "Lucky man," he said.

"If you say so."

Norman studied the woods along the shore, and higher up the outcrops and overlooks. The cove seemed a good place to calm whatever might be roiling inside, and he wondered if Gene cared that much about finding a good fishing spot. "So you're not at ArkMo anymore," he said. "Have you latched on somewhere else?"

"Like a tick, you mean?"

"That's not what I meant."

Gene shot a look that told Norman they'd crossed into new territory. "Three months, no work," he said, and brought the boat in a little closer to shore. He peered over the side as if hunting for sign, some riffle or faint current worthy of notice. "I better find something though. I've got a kid."

"You do?"

"A little boy," he said, motioning for another beer. When Norman hesitated, he stretched for the cooler himself, dragging it by his fingertips as the boat veered.

Norman felt a bit of his balance go and was grateful when Gene settled himself again at the wheel. Briefly his mind flashed on Nancy's hand drawings of the planned additions, two bedrooms, at least. "What's it like?" he asked. "Having a boy."

After a while Gene cut the engine. "You remember Shayla Gomes?"

Norman pictured a tall redhead who had been a standout on the volleyball team. "Sure," he said. "I remember her."

"Well, people change. Don't let anybody tell you different."

Norman took the comment in. "Shayla's the mother, then?"

"And father too, in her mind. She thinks they'll do fine without me."

Norman waited in the silence, felt it as a space that needed filling. "Maybe things will change when you're working again."

Turning, Gene nearly laughed in his face. "Keep dreamin', Teach."

Norman tried to keep the edge out of his voice. "I'm just saying things might look different by then."

"Sure. That's what they pay you for, right? To say. And say some more."

"You think I'm all talk?"

"You got a kid?"

"No."

"Well, teaching ain't the same as having, is it? School kids go home, you don't pay for them. You don't worry."

Norman saw no point in arguing. "Maybe so."

"I know so," Gene said. He started the boat and swung back toward the mouth of the cove, cutting so hard Norman had to brace himself against the side. The boat steadily increased speed, Norman sensing its power through his legs.

Ahead the cove widened, and Gene still accelerated. For a moment Norman thought of him as a runner pushing for home, sweeping past the coach's stop sign in his zeal to reach the plate. In the next moment Norman heard himself yelling "Boats," and then, from the periphery, he sensed the coming impact.

Norman shuddered at the memory, the car's steering wheel wet in his hands as he crested the long hill that brought his house into view. He was still picturing those frantic first glimpses of the wreckage, Gene nowhere in sight, when he drove past his own mailbox and saw Nancy rise from her flowerbed in the front yard, her arms spread as if asking where he thought he was going. He bit his lower lip and slowed, eventually turning into the Dickerson's driveway on the other side of the bend. Collisions on his mind, he checked the road carefully before backing out and heading toward home.

For dinner Nancy made spaghetti, indulging his request for extra slices of thickly slathered garlic bread while she watched him closely and shushed the girls whenever he spoke. Norman knew she was searching for any sign the pitch had done him harm, and he felt a twinge of guilt for having played the incident off as nothing more than a freak accident, something every umpire goes through if he works enough games. After they cleared the table and put the dishes in the washer, Norman let her follow him to their bedroom where he unbuttoned his shirt in front of the dresser mirror. The bruise was only marginally darker than when he'd showered two hours ago, but Nancy still gasped. She traced it with the tips of her fingers before gently slapping his cheek. "Next time you call me."

"Who says there'll be a next time?"

"You should get checked. Blows like that can alter heart rhythm."

"I'm not a kid."

"It doesn't happen just to kids. People can die from things like this."

He took her hand, placed the palm flat over his heart. "Just like normal," he said.

She frowned and leaned her ear to his chest, listening. She didn't straighten until she was sure. "All right," she said. "But if you start to feel something, you tell me."

"I will." He held up three fingers. "Scout's honor."

She pinched a love handle. "Come watch the Cardinals?"

"In a few minutes."

When she was gone Norman lowered himself to the foot of the bed and slowly buttoned his shirt, contemplating how hard a blow an event from fifteen years ago could still deliver. He thought of his own classes, where every semester he stood in front of twenty-five bored teenagers and insisted history wasn't a string of hand-me-down facts, but rather meaning they made with their minds. Few of his students showed much interest in the concept, but Norman had to admit that two years ago Cody Frazier had taken him at his word.

The assignment was to research some event that occurred anywhere in the Ozarks, the closer to Lotten or Bond County the better. Each student had to meet with Norman for topic approval, and one morning before class Cody walked in and slumped in a seat on the first row, directly in front of Norman's desk. He wore a ball cap pulled low over his forehead, and he carried a small rubber ball that he shifted from hand to hand, squeezing it in order to increase strength. Norman took out a writing tablet and settled himself behind his desk. "So what's on your mind? You come up with a topic?"

The boy sighed and bounced the ball a few times on the desk top. "I think so."

Norman noticed a nervous twitch in Cody's right leg, wondered why he hadn't spotted it before. "Well, what's the plan?"

"You're not gonna like it."

"Try me."

Again Cody sighed, but this time his head rose, his eyes steady beneath the cap brim. "I was thinking about researching that boat accident out at Catamount. The one that killed my father."

Without intending to, Norman sat back in his chair. As he did, he caught a narrowing of Cody's eyes. "That's quite a topic," he said.

"Then I can do it?"

Norman reached for a pen, found himself rough-sketching what looked like bluffs along the top margin of the page. "I'll have to think about it."

Cody leaned forward, the ball swallowed now in his right fist. "You said close to Lotten. It happened right out there at the lake."

Norman nodded and looked to the doorway. In the hall a few students were beginning to pass on their way to home rooms. "I'm not saying you shouldn't research this," he said. "No question you should. But I don't think I should be the one to oversee it."

"But you were there. And you're the teacher."

Norman rubbed his jaw, felt the faint scrape of whiskers on his palm. "Both those things together should tell you why I can't do this."

Cody rose and shoved the desk chair behind him, rattling the whole row. "That's just your way of telling me to drop it."

"No, it's not."

"You say."

"Look, it's my call. Once you get some distance on this, you'll understand."

"Sure. Everything will be just fine," Cody said, and started for the door. As he went he fired the rubber ball off the cement block wall. It was still dribbling around the floor as a few of Norman's first hour students entered the classroom and asked, laughing, what a bouncing ball had to do with history.

The bed springs creaked beneath Norman as he lay back and fingered his chest through the shirt cloth. Cody had never returned to class after that morning. For a time Norman had considered his transfer to the hamlet of Arditi a blessing, but now it threatened to discomfort him as much as his darkening bruise. Agitated, he got up and wandered into the living room, where Nancy and his youngest daughter Deana were exchanging high fives after a Yadier Molina home run. Smiling, he watched his family for a while before retreating to his tiny study, where he pulled out a telephone book. In the Arditi listings he found the number for an S. Gomes and wrote it down on the back of an old hardware store receipt. He studied the number, doodling a border of boats around the edges of the paper until he was satisfied he had come to a decision.

Slipping his phone into his shirt pocket, Norman quietly stepped out to the back yard and stood for a few minutes in the shade of the single oak. Even viewed from the back, his renovated house—expanded several times and re-clad now in new vinyl siding—stirred in him a sense of unmerited fortune. Taking a deep breath, he turned on his phone and hoped what he was about to do wouldn't be like a judgment call on the diamond, one that seemed right at the moment but bit hard for days after.

# His to Give

Stuck in traffic five cars back from the stoplight, Diane Drury turned the Malibu's air conditioner on high, hoping to coax a hint of cold air across her body. Nothing escaped the vents except a loud bluster. She shook her head, calculating that if she had stayed home yesterday instead of driving to Little Rock to locate her ex-husband, the car would still be under warranty. Ahead the light changed and she crowded the tailgate of a rusty pickup, an upended roll of wire fence tumbling in the truck bed. The old farmer behind the wheel showed no sign of hurry, jerking to a stop the moment the next light flashed yellow. Diane swerved into the turn lane to avoid rear-ending him and managed to get through the light, then into the proper lane again, without causing an accident. She was due at Sandra Pruitt's law office in ten minutes, and she meant to keep the appointment.

When she reached the town square, Diane circled twice to find a free parking spot. The lack of air conditioning made her skin feel gritty, and a thick heat followed her up the steps of Pruitt's rock-faced office, its narrow width squeezed between the Lotten Savings & Loan and the Ozark Grill. Inside the paneled lobby she motioned to the receptionist, who checked her calendar and nodded. Moments later a middle-aged man exited, trailed by a contrite-looking teenager wearing a Kid Rock T-shirt. Sandra Pruitt waved Diane in.

Pruitt was tiny and severely brunette, her waist narrow as a child's in the belted pant suits she wore daily like a uniform. This version was deep burgundy, with epaulettes that made her shoulders seem swallowed by material, but she'd earned a law degree at Ole Miss twenty years ago and built a reputation as the person to go to in Bond County if people thought they were in trouble. Now she glided behind her desk and tore the top sheet from a notepad. "Okay, Diane. What's up?"

Diane lowered herself into one of two tan wing chairs facing the desk. "Kevin's in Little Rock," she said. "With some woman."

Pruitt's eyebrows arched over round, black-rimmed glasses. "I assumed that. Is he working?"

"Probably. He could always find a job."

The notepad came at Diane from across the desk. "Write down the address. We'll get his wages."

Diane nodded, scribbling street and house number. When she finished she stared into the sliver of parking lot visible through Pruitt's narrowly parted curtains.

"Is that it?" Pruitt asked.

Diane inhaled deeply. The room seemed short of air. "I went there," she said. "To the house."

"What happened?"

"Nobody was home. I went in, though."

"Just like that?"

"Yes," she said, recalling how loose the rear screen had felt when she rattled the handle. The latch had popped open on her third try, giving as easily as a half-pulled nail. At the sound, an elderly black woman stepped out on the back stoop across the way, watching. "I'm his wife," Diane called, but the woman stared without expression. "We have a son. He won't pay support," she called, and finally the woman went inside, her own door closing softly.

Pruitt sighed as if she were in pain. "Did you take anything? Do any damage?"

Diane thought of the bedroom closet, Kevin's faded Levis and familiar shirts hanging next to blouses and skirts. Worn high tops lay where she knew they'd be, just beneath the bed. "He's made himself at home."

"That's not what I asked you."

The air conditioning droned quietly. "What if I took an old pocket knife? One he promised to Marcus."

"It's his to give, Diane."

"He won't pay a dime. Why does he get to choose what he'll give?"

Pruitt tapped sharp fingernails on the desktop. "Keep your mind on Marcus. I'll get your payments." She removed the round glasses. "Is that knife valuable? An antique or something?"

Diane shook her head. "Kevin's father carried it. It's all nicked up."

"A father to son thing."

"Yes." She took another deep breath before asking, "Did I ruin anything?"

Pruitt retrieved the notepad and replaced her glasses. "Maybe Kevin forgot to take that knife with him," she said. "You told me he travelled light when he left."

Diane felt too rueful to laugh. "I'm just afraid he'll do something."

"Like what? Has he ever hit you?"

"No. But he's mean other ways. He won't be forced."

"Mules can be made to move."

"This one's stubborn."

"They're all stubborn."

Outside, heat rose from the baking concrete. Diane dreaded the cauldron her car had become parked in the sun, so she walked to the dollar store down Jefferson Avenue. All week Marcus had been asking for a baseball, and though she considered him too young for the real thing, something soft and bouncy might be safe, yet still satisfy him. After examining a bin full of brightly colored rubber balls, she chose a white one with fake red stitches she judged a comfortable fit for his hand. At the check-out counter she broke her final ten, for once feeling calm about the diminished amount she deposited in her purse, as if exchanging one bill for several portended future solvency. Anyway, next year's teaching contract would be available in a few days.

When she returned to the square the Malibu was stifling. She cranked the windows open and headed back down Jefferson, across the railroad tracks to her sister's, where she turned into the sparsely graveled driveway and honked. Janet leaned out the front door, a phone cradled next to her ear, and jabbed an arm toward the back yard before disappearing inside.

"Marcus," Diane yelled, wondering if he would come without her having to drag him to the car. Lately he spent every allowable moment outside, either here with his cousins or roaming the patchy yard behind the duplex she had managed to rent. She yelled again, and finally he came shuffling around the corner of the house, his khaki shorts and white T-shirt bearing new grass stains. "You certainly stayed clean," she said as he plopped himself in the passenger seat. He nodded and pulled the fake baseball out of the store bag, examining the stitches closely.

"Do you like it?"

He shrugged, his shoulders hunching in a gesture eerily like his father's. Twice he bounced the ball off the glove compartment door before returning the ball to the plastic bag.

"You're welcome," Diane said, and punched the gas as she backed out of the driveway.

For dinner Diane made grilled cheese sandwiches, eating alone at the dinette while Marcus sat cross-legged in front of the television, lifting the sandwich to his mouth with one hand and working the remote with the other. When he finished he left his plate in the middle of the floor and bolted into the backyard. Diane started to call him back and make him carry the plate to the sink, but she couldn't summon enough will power. The duplex had only a window-unit air conditioner that blew from the living room toward the kitchen, and for what seemed a long time, she stayed still, absorbing the soothing stream.

Eventually she gathered the plates and ran soap and water over them at the sink. Outside she could see Marcus throwing his new ball as high as he could, trying to catch it as it came down. He missed each time, failing at a skill his father had made look effortless the last time Marcus saw him.

On that day it had been a yellow tennis ball. Diane was packing for the move to the duplex when Kevin surprised her by dropping by, actually helping clean out a couple of closets before taking Marcus outside for a game of catch. Twenty minutes later, as she opened the sliding glass door to yell that she could use more help, she spotted Kevin slinging the tennis ball as high as he could while Marcus stumbled after it in giddy circles, drunk on dizziness and delight.

"Catch it, boy," Kevin shouted, though the ball dropped ten feet behind Marcus and bounced as high as the roof.

Marcus tumbled sideways, giggling so hard he could barely stretch an arm to break his fall. Kevin began tickling Marcus while the boy squirmed.

"You'll make him wet his pants," Diane called, and suddenly Kevin looked up, flashing a grin that made her ache for better days.

"On your feet, boy," he ordered, lifting Marcus by the shirt collar. "Do this right for your mama." Snatching the ball, he took two quick strides and rifled the ball skyward. Marcus staggered beneath, his eyes locked on the ball as it climbed. When it began to drift behind him he backpedaled, losing his balance and covering his head as the ball came down several feet away. His father laughed and came to Diane in the doorway. "He'll never be a ball player."

"He's only six."

"You see an athlete out there?"

She pushed at him, but suddenly he lifted her into the house, closing the door behind him. She could feel the familiar comfort of his arms, and something more as his hands cupped her buttocks. "Stop."

"I thought you wanted help."

"Then carry those plates to the car. Be careful with them."

"I'm always careful."

Behind Kevin's shoulder she noticed Marcus, his forehead pressed against the glass door, the yellow tennis ball filling his hand. She shoved Kevin hard. "Stop playing. I need to be out of here by 1:00."

"Don't be so rough."

She went to the door and let Marcus in. "Let me have the ball, Marcus."

Marcus stepped away, hiding his hand behind his back. "It's mine," he said, and cut his eyes toward his father.

Reaching for him, Diane felt the boy's body tense. She looked to Kevin, who shrugged. "It's just a ball," he said.

She glared at him until he sighed and leaned down to Marcus. "Tell you what. Give me the ball, and when you visit me, we'll play."

"And where's he supposed to visit?"

Kevin ignored her, and Marcus stared at his shoes. Finally Kevin reached behind him and took the ball. "Now," he said, "everybody's happy."

Diane's face flushed warm. Marcus came closer, wrapping an arm around her legs. "Bye, Kevin," she said.

His laugh told her he thought she'd just thrown away a winning lottery ticket, on purpose. He ran a rough hand through his son's hair. "So long, Marco. See you soon."

That had been a year ago April. Since, there had been no calls or letters, no checks. Diane snapped a folded dish cloth on the counter and stepped outside, feeling the evening heat wrap her body like a towel. In the yard, Marcus was still heaving the ball, his brown bangs plastered to his forehead.

"Don't get too hot, Marcus."

"I'm not."

"Just a few more minutes. Then you need to come in and take a bath."

As usual, he pretended not to hear. After several more throws, she called, "So you like the new ball?"

He followed where it bounced toward the corner of the duplex. "I wanted a yellow one," he said.

Diane stepped back, swallowing. "It's not supposed to be yellow, Marcus."

Retrieving the ball, he drew back and angrily aimed a throw at the sky. "Yes it is," she heard him say.

Janet phoned moments after Diane managed to get Marcus out of the bathroom and into bed. Her voice was edgy, impatient. "What's going on with Kevin?"

"How should I know?"

"He called here. He wanted your address."

"Fine. Tell him to mail a check."

"He was out of your life, Diane. What did you do?"

"Me?"

"You. He seemed mad."

"It's his turn, don't you think?" There was a pause, and Diane imagined her sister chewing her thumbnail in frustration. "Just relax, okay."

"You're not going to talk to me, are you?"

"I'm talking to you now."

"Sure you are."

"What do you want me to say, Janet?"

"Just settle it, whatever it is. And don't put me in the middle." The phone beeped dead, Janet's way of adding an exclamation point.

*It's in the blood*, Diane thought, *needing that last word.* She pictured the final moment yesterday in Little Rock, after she'd already found the knife in the dresser drawer. The only necessary thing was to leave the bedroom and keep walking. Instead, she let her hand close on the tube of lipstick and scrawl across the mirror, "You owe him the knife." She didn't bother to sign her name.

Behind her, from the direction of Marcus's room, Diane became aware of a pounding sound, evenly spaced. She hurried down the hall and burst in, finding Marcus standing at the foot of his bed. He was throwing the fake baseball against the wall.

"What do you think you're doing?" she yelled. "You're supposed to be asleep."

For a moment he looked frightened. Then he rolled his shoulders in that passive, infuriating shrug.

Diane moved close and stood over him, grateful for the difference in their heights. "You'll ruin the plaster that way. Give me the ball."

Reluctantly, he passed it into her hand.

"Now get back in bed, Marcus."

Slowly he did so, rolling onto his side and turning his back to her. She was a full two steps out of his room when she heard him call.

Taking a deep breath, she returned to the doorway. "What now?"

His back was still turned. "I guess white's okay."

She nodded and walked unsteadily toward the living room, one hand against the wall, as if she'd just been offered the world.

# TRAVELING MERCIES

Ray Denton first noticed the catch in his fuel line an hour northwest of Memphis, but he continued on, hoping he could make it across the river into the city before the worrisome slip in the car's power became too serious. Not once in his life had he broken down along a highway, and he told himself, mantra-like, that his luck would hold. Twenty minutes later the engine began firing so intermittently he barely made it to the exit ramp outside Ajax, Arkansas, a town he thought he might have stopped in once for fuel. Leaning close to the steering wheel, he coaxed the Impala off the ramp into a thin stream of Thursday afternoon traffic, but the engine cut out again, the whole vehicle shuddering maddeningly before slowing to a crawl. Soon cars began to swerve around him, forcing him to pull onto the narrow shoulder. When he opened his door a crack, a horn blared through like a punch in his ear.

Flinching, Ray looked at the cell phone on the seat beside him. He'd never joined AAA and knew no one to call in Ajax. For a moment he considered dialing his office

at Ozark Mountain Community College, where he was
Dean, but there was nothing Fern, his assistant, could do
from a hundred miles away. Ahead he spotted a Wendy's
sign, and beyond that what looked like a service station.
Slipping the phone in his pocket, he glanced at his new suit
stretched across the back seat and then down at his freshly
shined loafers before stepping cautiously onto the blacktop.
A hot wind blew past, and he hurried to the front of the
Impala while a pickup pounded by, buffeting him in its
wake. By the time he reached the Wendy's parking lot his
shirt was damp, sweat pooling over his eyebrows, but Ajax
Automotive lay just ahead.

Heavy odors of grease and gasoline spoiled the air as
Ray approached the three-bay garage, where somewhere
in back a steely tool pinged off concrete. In the first bay a
mechanic rattled the loose muffler of a blue sedan before
stepping directly beneath the undercarriage for a better
look. Ray shuddered, imagining the rack buckling, the car
coming down on the mechanic's body.

"Help you?" barked a heavy-set man. Grateful for the
offer, Ray followed the man's wave as he motioned toward
an open door. Once inside Ray found no place to sit, only a
counter and cash register, the back wall lined with shelves
of chips and candy bars. The man settled himself behind
the counter and scratched a salt-and-pepper goatee. A name
patch with a red *Stan* embroidered in cursive perched like
a miniature billboard above his chest pocket.

"My car died back there," Ray said. "I think it could be
the fuel line."

Stan rolled a wrist, checking his watch. "We can tow it.
Maybe get you going in the morning."

Ray groaned. "I need to get to my hotel. I have a job
interview tomorrow, in Memphis."

Stan said nothing, and Ray recognized the glazed

inattention he often associated with Walmart cashiers and supermarket clerks, employees he assumed endured each shift wishing only to get home to families and television sets. He turned and studied the Wendy's across the way, where people in dependable vehicles idled in the drive-through lane. "What's the chance of a ride?"

Stan shrugged. "Trace might do it after we close. I'll check when he pulls your car."

Ray handed over his keys. Outside he blinked into the sun and waited by the gas pumps. Soon the Impala glided in behind a shiny red and white wrecker, *Ajax Automotive* painted prominently on the doors. Stan met the driver and jabbed a thumb in Ray's direction, gesturing toward the highway as he talked. When Stan finished and retreated to the garage, the driver gave Ray half a wave. Ray approached, guessing the man to be thirty or so, noting the blond stubble that shadowed his face. A faded Memphis Redbirds cap counterpointed a blue work shirt and matching trousers, both streaked with grime.

"Trace Shipley," the man said. "Sounds like you're having some trouble."

"I'm afraid so. My car died."

"Yeah. Pinches when your rig breaks down."

Ray pointed back toward the garage. "Your boss? He said you might take me on to Memphis. I can pay."

Trace sighed and stared at an oily patch of concrete as if something in the stain worried him. When he looked up, his forehead was furrowed. "Think you could spare a hundred?" he asked. "I'm not trying to screw you. It's just if we get caught in traffic, I'll miss my boy's Little League game. He's pitching."

Ray met the man's wide, blue eyes and briefly wondered how to tell a Samaritan from a serial killer. "A hundred's fine," he said.

◆  ◆  ◆

Trace's personal vehicle resembled a farm truck that had seen better days, its cream paint peeling along the hood and passenger door, an impressive dent rusting above the right rear wheel well. Ray settled his overnight bag in the middle of the seat, but there was no place to hang his suit so he folded it gently and held it on his knees like a pie bound for the county fair.

"We'll hit rush hour in West Memphis," Trace said, starting the engine to a radio blast of country music, which he punched off with the flat of his hand. "But once we're over the river there'll be more people heading out than going in."

Ray nodded, relieved to be traveling once again in the direction of his hotel room where he could hang up his suit, stretch on the bed, and collect his thoughts for tomorrow's interview at Western Tennessee. He'd need to call Teresa too. His wife wasn't thrilled about the possibility of moving to a big city like Memphis, but she hadn't made herself sick with worry either. Ray knew she doubted he'd be hired as Dean of Developmental Studies, since she thought the position too big a jump for him. *They've never heard of Ozark Mountain*, she'd said when he first told her he planned to apply. *Or you.* Then last week, when he announced he'd made the interview round, she pursed her lips as a first defense against bad news and asked how many applicants had received the same invitation. After he finally admitted he didn't know, her face relaxed into a hint of a smile. Ray concluded she was imagining a large room crowded with mid-level administrator types, all crammed shoulder-to-shoulder.

The pickup merged into traffic, and a moment later a kick of acceleration settled Ray deeply into his seat. Trace flipped the turn signal and powered past a matronly lady and two young children in a Ford Escape. "We'll get you where you're going," he said, his voice solemn as a minister's.

Ray considered the speedometer, its needle rising rapidly. "No need to hurry. They'll hold my room."

Trace nodded and lifted the Redbirds cap by the bill, rubbing his forehead with the heel of his palm. A thinning hairline made him look older, more careworn than Ray first thought. "Just like to do a job right," he said.

Ray watched the speedometer settle at seventy. "That's a good quality."

Trace glanced his way. "Stan said you're looking for work. Might have a line in Memphis."

"An interview," Ray corrected. "I'm thinking it may be time for a change."

Trace smiled into the windshield. "Time for a change," he repeated, lilting the words as if they came from a favorite song. "We all get to that place, don't we?"

Ray looked down the long, flat highway, the last of Ajax's commercial properties giving way on either side to the green of cultivated fields. Back in Bond County those fields would be pastures, horses and beef cattle dotting stony hills and steep ridges, the thin soil too stingy to nurture crops that grew in orderly, prospering rows. He thought a moment of his older brother Dale, who for years had worked full-time factory jobs, jumping at any overtime he could get just to hold onto eighty acres— hard land that had already cost him a wife, a John Deere tractor, and a back that bent without pain. Ray shook his head, wondering if the choice to stay home and build a career at Ozark Mountain had cost him just as much. "No change, no life," he said, and immediately sensed Trace give him a quick, assessing stare.

Thirty minutes later they crested a hill on the far side of West Memphis and spotted the bridge silvering in the sun. "Here we go," Trace said. "Big ol' Muddy."

Ray straightened as if he were being measured for height. Craning his neck, he waited for a glimpse of the river while Trace swept past an overburdened gravel truck to improve their entry onto the two-lane bridge. Ray had crossed the Mississippi at least a dozen times before, but now he felt a fluttering in his stomach and thought, briefly, of a bird lifting from the ground.

As always, Ray was surprised at how quickly the river could be crossed. He counted several barges in the distance and listened to the pounding of the pickup's tires, noting with satisfaction the small boundary marker in the middle of the bridge that told him Arkansas was behind him. Then they were on the other side, surging into the hurly-burly of Memphis itself.

"So where's your hotel?" Trace called over the traffic. "You'll need to point me."

Ray fumbled in his chest pocket for the directions he'd printed from his computer and noticed Trace glancing his way, eyebrows arched. "Mapquest," Ray said.

Trace swallowed, his Adam's apple rising and falling. "Okay. Fire away."

Ray spent the next few minutes glancing between the computer's directions and the city's signs, calling out exit numbers and street names until the traffic finally thinned and they needed only to navigate one stoplight and a right turn into the parking lot of the Fairmont Inn. He was swiveling his head, hoping the university might be close enough to glimpse, when Trace slammed the brakes and rocked him toward the dashboard. The seatbelt grabbed him with a jolt as a blue blur of SUV surged out of a side street, claiming the pickup's front fender in a groaning complaint of metal. Wide-eyed, Ray watched the SUV shudder across the opposite lane and nose onto the shoulder.

"Hell Fire!" Trace yelled, anger ricocheting around the cab.

Ray checked over his shoulder, fearful they might be plowed from the rear, but he saw only a handful of halted vehicles, their shocked drivers pantomiming behind sun-stippled windshields. Slumping back around, he noticed with a pang that his suit had been flung to the floorboard, his own loafers now pressing footprints into the lapels.

Trace gripped him by the shoulder, each finger a prong. "Are you hurt?"

"No. You?"

"I'm shorn a front end, that's for sure." Jumping down from the cab, Trace snatched off his cap and studied the damage until anxious drivers began to honk and crowd into the next lane, determined to pass. Exasperated, he waved them on before returning and leaning in the window. "Steer over to the shoulder, okay? I need to check on that other guy."

Ray watched him pick through traffic, then moved behind the wheel, cautiously guiding the truck to the shoulder in a slow roll that sounded like tin cans dragging from the driveshaft. He shut off the engine and stepped down amid a litter of flung glass and popped rivets, the sun instantly heating one side of his face. Across the way, Trace helped an old man out of the SUV and steadied him against the side of the vehicle. The man kept shaking his head and talking with his hands, eventually beginning to weep. Trace gave him a couple of stiff pats on the back, then reached into his pocket and brought out a handkerchief, passing it into the old man's hands. Moments later he returned to retrieve his phone from the cab and report the accident. "I don't think he knows where he is," he told Ray. "He keeps saying they moved the stop sign on him."

Ray wondered if the man had dementia, or maybe just heat stroke. For the second time today he was sweating through his shirt, and when he turned to take in the Fairmont in the distance, the marquee shimmered with the promise of air conditioning and cable television. Immediately Ray considered handing Trace the money they had agreed on and hiking the rest of the way.

"They ought to be here soon," Trace said, ending the call. "I told them the old guy's pretty frazzled." Motioning toward the hotel, he flicked an invisible pebble over Ray's head. "There she is. You're in walking distance, at least."

Ray nearly reached for his wallet. "What about you?"

Trace let out a sigh. "Right now I got to deal with this mess. Talk to the cops, see if they can help me get a tow." He drew a forearm across his slick brow. "There goes Trey's game. He'll probably throw a no-hitter now, won't he?"

For the first time Ray remembered Trace's son. "How old is he?"

"Ten. Pretty good arm." Suddenly Trace caught a pulse of energy and leaned close, his voice confiding. "I'm partial though."

Nodding, Ray recalled attending a few of Michelle's middle school volleyball games. Mostly she had sat on the bench, playing only when a match became lop-sided, and even then she moved around the court tentatively, as if she preferred her teammates to control the action. Ray assumed she'd tried out merely because it was something to do, a way to be with her friends. He hadn't enjoyed the shrill shouting from some of the parents and was glad when Michelle quit after only one season, but years later she made a strange remark at the dinner table after qualifying for state competition in oral interpretation. He had asked what time her first round would be, so that he could drive down to Little Rock to hear her speech. "Don't bother, Daddy," she'd said. "You'll just be bored." When he protested, she and Teresa rolled their eyes at each other, and he felt a certain relief that he wasn't included. Yet his daughter's words had lodged like a cyst beneath the skin.

The sun poured down in a steady blast, and Ray decided he was wasting time. "I appreciate the ride," he said, pulling out his wallet. On impulse, he added an extra ten. "For your trouble."

Slowly Trace raised the bill of his cap with his thumb. "You can go broke paying for folks' troubles," he said.

Ray continued to hold out the ten. "It's the least I can do."

After a few seconds Trace took the extra bill and handed Ray the overnight bag and rumpled suit from the truck cab. Ray nodded and started for the hotel, anxious for the cool quiet of his room. The walk was longer than he anticipated and several times he shifted the bag from one hand to the other, fearful the suit would wrinkle more severely with each jostle.

Inside the lobby he waited at the reception desk until a young woman emerged from a back room and apologized while scanning her computer screen. At first she couldn't locate his reservation, and for an awful moment he wondered if Western had canceled the interview at the last minute. Then the girl's face brightened. "You're here after all," she declared, legitimizing him with duplicate key cards and directions to the elevator.

His room lay at the end of the hall on the second floor and smelled vaguely of dry-cleaning. He hung the suit in the bathroom and let the shower run hot, counting on steam to remove wrinkles. After downing a soda from the hall vending machine, he collapsed on the bed to phone home. Teresa picked up on the fifth ring.

He left out the car trouble and the wreck itself, telling her only that he'd arrived safely, that he was looking forward to the interview. "I think I have a shot," he said, although the sentiment sounded thin when he heard it from his own lips.

"Okay." Her voice was so flat he imagined her stretching an arm to inspect her fingernails. "Oh," she said. "Michelle went out tonight."

"What?"

"A movie. With Tony Edmonds."

Ray ground his teeth. He tried to recall anyone named Tony Edmonds and finally settled on a thin, mildly acned boy whose shyness offered hope Michelle would lose interest quickly. He didn't feel up to the complications his daughter's heart might engender, especially if things worked out with Western. "I meet the search committee at 11:00 tomorrow," he said.

Teresa made a sound as if she'd been sucker punched. "Then why did you go down there tonight?"

"What else would I do?"

"You could have left in the morning. You'd have plenty of time."

Ray massaged his eyelids and wished for sleep. "I have meetings scheduled from 8:00 on. I told you that."

"No you didn't."

"I'm sure I did."

Her voice lowered, took on an edge. "You're always so sure."

Pushing himself to a sitting position, he flattened his back against the headboard. "I have to stay focused, Teresa. Let's not start this again. I don't need it."

"What you don't need is that job. None of us do."

Anger surged him off the bed. "Don't start the 'us' games, okay. I've had my fill."

"What 'us'? You're the one that's off in Memphis."

"I'm trying for something better."

"For you. Nobody else wants it."

"Because you only want what you want, everything else be damned."

Her voice came higher now, wavering. "I'm not the selfish one."

"So I guess that leaves me, doesn't it?"

"You always do this."

"Do what? Keep you from running my life? It's mine. I get to choose."

Her voice was so muffled now he couldn't make out her reply, only the clear, precise click as she ended the call.

An hour later Ray sat at a bistro table in a Subway one block behind the Fairmont. He'd ordered a Spicy Italian but had finished less than half the sandwich, his nerves so jangled the food seemed an assault on his stomach. Little had gone the way he'd planned for this trip, and he knew he had to turn things around for tomorrow. Probably the best thing would be to go back to the hotel and relax, find some way to get Teresa's nonsense out of his head. At the very least, he ought to review his notes a final time.

Outside the air had cooled a bit, the evening pleasant enough he decided to cut across the grassy knoll separating the Fairmont from the strip of shops and fast food stores. He was huffing a bit by the time he made it to the top and stepped onto the parking lot, which was nearly empty. There he noticed only a young man standing near the trunk of a sports car, fishing for keys in the deep front pocket of his cargo shorts. Ray nodded in passing and heard a musical clink as the other man lifted the keys in a casual, acknowledging wave. A few steps nearer the building and Ray registered a rushing glissando in the air behind his right ear, too late to duck the blow that robbed him of his legs and sent him lurching toward the pavement.

Unable to keep his balance, he struck the asphalt in waves, elbows and chest first, then jaw and eye socket in a stunning jolt that bounced his head as if his neck were a spring. Instinct told him to rise, but his assailant's knee dropped like a dumbbell between his shoulder blades and he flattened, lying still even as his wallet was jerked from his back pocket. Much later he managed to push himself upward into a pained, unsteady crouch, and then to a cautious posture he thought of as vertical. When he reached to check the empty pocket, his hand grasped only a thready remnant of cloth, which he let flutter to the ground.

The journey to the hotel entrance seemed immeasurable now, his face burning and throbbing at the same time. When he finally arrived at the front door he leaned his weight against the glass and stumbled inward, only to see the front desk again unoccupied. Halted, he wondered whether his aching jaw was broken, whether he could call for help with anything resembling human sound.

From his right appeared a man in soiled blue, face blurred beneath a red cap until the face shaped itself into a likeness Ray knew. "I got you, Bud," Trace was saying. "Let's just slide over to this chair." Ray felt strong arms guiding him, lowering him to cushioned fabric, and when he leaned back, his head cradled comfortingly in the corner of a wing chair. He let his eyes close.

"What happened to you, man? Stay awake now."

Ray willed his eyelids open. He saw Trace had shoved the cap high on his shining head. "Bastard robbed me," he mumbled, and felt something wet leak from his mouth.

Trace drove him to the hospital in the loaner from the insurance company, and by the time they arrived Ray's swimmy head had begun to clear. His insurance card was lost with his wallet, but the emergency room staff bandaged his scrapes and checked him for concussion syndrome. After a couple of hours under observation he was released, and Trace led him out onto the well-lit parking lot. Ray still felt jumpy at the hint of any shadow and was thankful for another body at his side. Only then did he think to ask why Trace had returned to the hotel.

"Just thought I should check on you," he said. "Make sure you had a way back tomorrow."

A low breeze scraped an empty Doritos bag across their path, and Ray suddenly realized he'd made no arrangements beyond the interview. He wasn't even sure he wanted to go through with it now. "I've got no plans," he said. "The ones I had look shot to hell."

Trace opened the passenger side door and held it for him while Ray folded in one sore limb at a time. As they left the parking lot and merged into traffic, Ray studied Trace's profile, considered how long the man's day had been. "You're heading home tonight, I guess?"

Trace shrugged. "I could probably find a room somewhere, stay over till after your thing tomorrow. Stan owes me some time."

Ray's mood turned a deeper blue, and he wondered what might move him to make the same offer to a stranger, even someone closer. He recalled an incident last fall when he'd let Teresa fend for herself after a water pipe had broken in the basement and he didn't want to run out on a meeting with the college president. She'd barely spoken to him for a week after that, leaving his dinners on the stove and keeping her distance as if one touch from his hand might scald her skin. The memory turned something in his stomach, and by the time the Fairmont marquee came into sight he realized he could summon no energy for tomorrow's interview. Perhaps if Western allowed him to re-schedule he could kindle his enthusiasm again, but he doubted it. "No need to wait on me," he said. "I'll go whenever you're ready."

They parked near the entrance, and Ray could feel Trace's steady gaze. "You sure? What about needing a change and all that?"

Ray shifted painfully in his seat. "I do," he said. "But this isn't the place for it."

Trace lifted the cap and raked fingers through what was left of his hair. "I can hear that," he said. "You want to leave now?"

Ray thought about the call he would need to make to Teresa, how he'd have to tell her about the car, and being robbed, even ask her to drive a hundred miles through the dark to Ajax. For a moment his chest constricted, but then he realized she would go to such lengths for him, even tonight. He swallowed and turned his face to the glass. "Just let me have a couple of minutes," he told Trace. "Then I'll be ready to go home."

# Punch List

A rt Pyatt swallowed the first bite of his wife's lasagna just as the Roberts woman called. A moment later Ann Marie brought the phone to the kitchen table, her eyebrows arched. "She sounds upset," she said, uncovering the receiver and handing him the phone. Art took a deep breath, inhaling the aroma of home-made pasta sauce and feeling Ann Marie's fingers settle on his shoulder. The call, he knew, would be about David.

As soon as he said hello, Regina Roberts filled his ear with complaints. "Your grandson still hasn't finished the punch list," she said, biting off each word. "I've called him three times in the last week. He came today, but as best I can tell he wasted forty-five minutes puttering. He still hasn't bolted those bookcases to the wall in the den, and there are three rooms without covers for light switches. I have grandchildren, Arthur. He knows that."

Art eyed the casework in his eat-in kitchen, every cabinet framed, faced, stained by his own hands. He sighed. "If you'll be home this evening I'll come myself, make sure everything gets finished."

Ann Marie pinched his shoulder but Art waved her off, continuing to listen through the long silence. Finally Regina Roberts spoke. "I'll be here," she said. "I know you're trying to delegate, but this has gone on long enough."

"I agree."

"All right then."

She hung up and Art set the phone next to his plate. His wife stood over him, arms crossed. "Eat," she commanded, then stalked to the living room and mashed the volume control on the television remote. Applause from *Wheel of Fortune* invaded the kitchen like a mock cheer.

Distracted, Art ate without tasting his food. In his mind's eye he could see David at the Roberts job, shoulders stiff with resentment that he'd been called back to a task that no longer interested him, one he didn't care to finish. Art shook his head and tossed down a handful of blood pressure pills before rinsing his plate at the sink. "Be back by dark," he called toward the living room, where Ann Marie sat with a crocheted pillow clutched to her waist. He left by the back door, settling into the soiled truck cab he might as well call a second home. Swinging onto the highway, he rolled down the window and let the air of an Ozark evening buffet him softly. The Roberts house was at the north end of the county, maybe two miles from the Missouri line. He told himself he should try to enjoy the drive.

Twenty minutes later the view of a neatly fenced pasture with cattle dotting a cleared ridge reminded him that he liked the land up this way, the soil a little richer because of the river. Over the years he'd built three houses along this road, and after tonight he'd count the Roberts place as his fourth, the sixty-fifth overall. It was a big brick and stone two-story, set back from the highway and accessed by a gravel drive that wound through the woods. The house had taken Art and his three-man crew, plus David, a good sixteen months to build, and there had been the usual tensions, like the time Regina Roberts decided she didn't like the curve of the stairway Art had drawn up. She let the boys finish roughing it in before telling him she wasn't satisfied, and Art exchanged words with her about that. Overall, though, she'd been a fair woman to work for. He had no complaint about her calling tonight and blamed himself for not keeping a closer check on David. He knew what he knew about his grandson.

A light rain had passed through, the highway pavement still wet as Art turned onto the gravel drive and felt a wall of muggy air invade the truck cab. He drove on into the woods until the view opened onto a cleared pasture and a wide yard sown in zoysia grass, the house planted like a spike in the empty lawn. He'd tried to talk Regina Roberts into saving some of the larger oaks and hickories as yard trees, but she'd been determined to start her landscaping from scratch.

Art was particularly proud of this house. To his eye he'd built prettier ones—solid, symmetrical homes with wide porches or columned porticoes—but this one Regina Roberts had encouraged him to draw up on his own, without depending on commercial house plans or architectural blueprints. She'd wanted something resembling French Country, with a complicated roofline and dormers of different sizes and shapes, but after studying twenty or thirty dog-eared examples from her magazines and plan books, Art told her he thought he could sketch out something she might like. It took him several days, and she didn't fall in love with his first sketch, but they kept talking. After his fourth try she peered at him over her reading glasses and said, "I like your eye. That's why I called you in the first place. I like the way you see."

"So you want me to build it?"

"Yes, I do. Build me this house," she said, tapping Art's sketch three times with the rim of her glasses.

Art had built the house she wanted, or so he told himself as he parked, cinched his tool belt, and started up the walkway toward the walnut-stained front door. He knocked three times and the door swung open, Regina Roberts waving him into her tiled entryway. She spoke his name as her only greeting and led him down the hall to the den, where she had installed a couch, a rug, and two burgundy wing chairs. Several boxes stuffed with books cluttered the floor.

Art gestured toward the nearest bookcase. "I shouldn't be more than twenty minutes."

"Good," she said, her heels receding on hardwood as she walked to the other end of the house. When she was out of earshot Art took a closer look at David's work. Two of the cases were fine, the dark screws flush against the cherry finish, but the rest of the cases were in haphazard condition, a bewildering array of screws left dangling from their starter holes. The final case lacked any screws at all, only pencil scratches to mark where holes should be drilled. To stave off a headache, Art pinched the bridge of his nose.

For the next half hour he worked in the den, finishing the cases and double-checking each one, assuring himself he hadn't overlooked more of David's carelessness. Then he went through the house installing pewter light switch covers, grateful when he tapped the head of his screw on the final one, its scrolled edging and floral design masking the rough-cut hole stuffed with wires and switches.

He found Regina Roberts sipping wine at her breakfast table as she gazed into the woods bordering her back yard. "All finished," he said.

"Thank you, Arthur." She stood to face him. "I'm sorry I was brusque."

He waved her words away. "You had a right."

Carefully, she placed the wine glass on a coaster. "I was worried. About the light switches especially. My grandchildren are at that age."

"Mine's grown, but he still acts like a kid."

She smiled. "I seem to remember David working for his father."

"He didn't learn much there. Bobby throws houses up like tents."

"Is he still in Jonesboro?"

"Mostly. Plus a couple of crews in Memphis. Anywhere there's an empty lot."

"At least he has work."

"At least."

She stepped back—away from his gruffness, Art sensed, away from the chance he'd let spill the family toxin. He made a sweeping motion with his arm, taking in the room. "Glad for the chance," he said. "You were good to work for."

Her eyes seemed to assess the room's details—the deep tray ceiling, the hand-stained French doors. "I'm grateful, Arthur. I truly am."

His cheeks warmed. Turning, he tipped an invisible cap. "I know the way out," he said, making his way through the kitchen and entry hall to the substantial front door, which opened easily before closing crisply behind him.

Outside he noticed the late August sun lowering against the tree tops, a glow crowning the western ridge. *Pretty*, he thought, though he no longer drove so well in light like this. He stood for a moment with his hand on the door handle of his pickup, dreading the way glare hid curves from him and blinded him on hilltops. Then he slid behind the wheel and lowered the visor, reminding himself that dread never solved anything. He would have to let David go, had known it since Regina Roberts called. He might as well tell the boy tonight.

David's trailer court was at the far end of Lotten, a good twenty miles to the southwest. When Art reached town he circled the square, glancing at the 1893 courthouse and turning onto Jefferson Avenue toward the railroad tracks. There he passed through a section of rundown clapboard houses people had once called Sambo Hill. At the crest he negotiated a narrow cross street and pulled into the trailer court, where two rows of six trailers sat in a patch of gravel. After a moment he spotted his grandson's dented pickup parked behind the final trailer in the back row.

Mounting the jerrybuilt stoop, he knocked before entering a living room barely wider than a good-sized hall. The room held one chair, paired with a brown couch shoved beneath a single window. "David," he shouted. "It's Pop."

After a while David came down the hall and poked a wet head into the room. "Hey."

"We have to talk."

"About what?"

"You."

"Give me a sec."

Art grunted. The low ceiling made him feel he was about to scrape his head. "David," he yelled again.

David came back buttoning a pair of jeans. At the refrigerator he grabbed a can of Mountain Dew and flopped on the couch. "So what's up?"

Art lowered himself to the edge of the chair and searched for words. "The Roberts place," he finally said. "You didn't finish the punch list."

David set the unopened can on an end table. "That won't take long."

"It should have been done already. Two weeks ago when I asked."

"All right. Tomorrow."

"I did it myself. Just now."

David rolled his eyes. "I told that woman I'd take care of her damn list. She wouldn't stop calling."

Art felt a sudden urge to rise, put hands on his grandson. "You're derelict, David. I can't have that."

"I'm not gonna be at her beck and call, Pop. That's no way to live."

"You'll have to find a way. You've put in your last day with me."

"Seriously? Over this?"

"Over not doing a thing I've asked the last year."

David stood to his full height. "You said I had a share. 'Come home,' you said. 'Learn to take over.'"

"If you proved yourself. But you didn't. Now I have to find somebody I can hand off to."

"And it won't be Dad, will it?"

"No, it won't."

David wagged a finger. "You know what this is about? All of it? It's you thinking you're the only one that knows anything."

Art stood. "All you had to do was finish the punch list!"

"Screws, Pop! Light covers. That's all it was."

"It was your job! And you didn't finish."

David moved toward the kitchen. "Dad said nobody could work for you. I should've listened." Then he disappeared down the hallway.

Art started to follow, part of him wishing to smooth the boy's feelings, another part wanting to push, shove, maybe batter. Instead he stalked outside where the evening had passed into dusk, only a faint afterglow rimming roofs at the bottom of the hill. He drove slowly, his foot lightly riding the brake as he coasted down toward the square, where he found only a handful of cars parked outside McFarland's, lawyers and court clerks lingering after dinner. Unready to face Ann Marie's questions, he pulled into a parking spot where he could rest his eyes on the courthouse.

The architect, Scrimshire, was only nineteen when he rode from St. Louis with plans already drawn—plans that called for three stories of red brick lit by matching rows of arched windows, atop it all a vaguely Gothic roof that sported three dormers to a side. Art admired Scrimshire's pluck to propose such a building for a town bushwhackers had burned to a crisp only thirty years before, not a soul left in Bond County by the end of the war. Scrimshire had even stayed to oversee construction, feuding daily with the contractor and town fathers who together preferred slap dash and shortcut. Eventually he managed to impose his will, installing a crew of black bricklayers and hod carriers hired from Oxford, Mississippi, their hands the instruments of his vision.

Art had seen creased, faded photographs of those Mississippi men, even knew one to be great-grandfather to the bricklayer Jude Foster. Jude worked for himself, but he had bricked nearly half of Art's houses. Art thought a moment about Jude's two sons, trying to remember whether either had kept a hand in construction. A pain went through him when he realized he hadn't seen them in years. Removing his glasses, he rubbed a handkerchief over the lenses and pictured the rock house behind Barbara Bond Cemetery where Jude had raised his boys. He decided to swing by and see if Jude would do one more house for him.

The cemetery was just off the highway two miles west of town, bookended now by a Shell station on one side and a ramshackle building called Hillbilly Antiques on the other. Art circled behind the cemetery and pulled into a narrow gravel drive, spotting Jude's F-150 parked beside the shed. He got out and followed the stepping stones to the stoop, admiring the way Debby Foster's geraniums overflowed their pots.

Jude came to the door in his sock feet, his shirt unbuttoned. "Art," he said. "Something wrong?"

Art eyed Jude's feet and shook his head, regretting his presumption. "Time got away from me, Jude. I'll phone tomorrow."

Jude looked back into the living room, where Debby raised a cup and called, "Come in, Art. Have some coffee."

Again he shook his head. "It's too late, Debby. I'll call another time." She protested politely as he moved away from the stoop, and halfway down the path he heard Jude clomping behind him, work boots untied. "Wait up, Art. I'll walk you."

At the truck Jude shook out a cigarette. Art waited until he lit up and had his first puff. "I've bid on a house out by the river," he said. "We'll be past the rains by the time I need brick. If it stays warm, you could work steady."

Jude leaned against the hood, his top-heavy body forcing a groan from the metal. Looking away, he traced the arc of an eyebrow with his thumb. "I turned sixty-five a couple months ago. Pretty much promised we'd retire."

Art hooked a heel on the bumper. "Sixty-five's in my rearview."

Jude muffled a smoker's laugh. "I noticed you didn't pay much attention to it."

"Tried not to. But now I'm short a man on the crew."

Jude studied him. "Your grandson?"

Hearing the question made Art feel like an old balloon leaking air. "You must have seen that coming."

"He don't want to be here, Art. I went through it with mine."

Art looked out at the cemetery, the stones washed now in moonlight. Suddenly he remembered the time Jude awoke to the sounds of white teenagers partying among the graves and fired two shotgun blasts above their heads, scattering them like quail. He'd made the front page of the *Ledger* for that. Art cleared his throat and motioned toward the cemetery. "Looks like you're still keeping the place up."

"Somebody has to," Jude said, flicking away his cigarette.

Art watched the glow fade in the gravel. "I remember your daddy. I think maybe your granddaddy."

"He's over there in the corner. Passed before I was born."

Art contemplated the seven or eight stones marking Jude's family. "You gonna lay near them?"

Jude shook his head. "She got us a couple of plots at Oak Valley." He tapped out another cigarette and lit it. "Nobody's been buried here for years."

Out on the highway, cars trailed the sounds of their passing. At the Shell station a semi eased out of the lot, the driver readying for the night's haul. Art felt prodded by motion. "I wish you'd sleep on that retirement business a night or two," he said. "Maybe let me know in a couple of days."

After a while Jude nodded. "Surely."

Art held out his hand and they shook. "It was good to see Debby. Tell her so."

"I will."

Back in the truck Art circled the way he had come, wondering how many graves he was passing that lacked even a stone, their presence known only to Jude.

Nearing the bypass, he left the highway and went through town slowly. He wasn't sure what words he would have for Ann Marie, but he would need them. She'd ask why he'd been gone so long, and what his plans were for David.

Approaching the house, he saw the porch light from the road. Ann Marie always turned it on when he was out past sundown, but tonight he would have preferred to climb the steps in darkness. At least she didn't meet him at the door, which gave him a chance to draw a full glass of water from the faucet before she padded in barefoot and took a seat at the kitchen table.

"Thought you might be asleep," he said.

"No you didn't."

He sat down and took a long drink. "I finished at the Roberts place."

"Are you tired?"

"A little."

"You should take off early tomorrow."

"I'll think about it."

She crossed her arms. "What about David?"

Art finished his water and studied the grain of the table through the clear bottom of the glass, the droplets wavering his vision only a little. "I let him go," he said.

Ann Marie stiffened, a rigidity he felt across the table. "What will he do?"

"Head back to Jonesboro I imagine."

Her breathing quickened. "You know he and Bobby aren't getting along."

"Right now him and me aren't best friends either."

"You need to fix that."

"Don't put this on me. He didn't do the work."

"Then talk to him. Make him hear you."

"Mama, he's twenty-five. What he needs to hear he's already been told, by me and others."

"Then tell him again."

Art looked at her, pain deepening the wrinkles on her face, puffing the skin under her eyes, above the cheeks. He reached for her hand, caught the last two fingers before she could pull away. "I want what you want," he said. "But things are broke I don't know how to fix."

She dropped her eyes to the table top, let her free hand fall to her lap. "Maybe you're broke too."

He sat back, her hand no longer in his. "What's that mean?"

She snatched his glass from the table and carried it to the dishwasher, jamming it over a prong and letting it clink against the other dishes. "You can fire him as a helper. Not as your grandson."

"I know that."

"You say you do, but you fired Bobby and he's never come back. Now you're doing the same to David."

"It's not the same."

"Tell me how it's different."

His mind blanked except for a vision of Scrimshire's courthouse, the arched, matching windows. "They've got their own minds," he said. "I can't make them line up like I want."

She gave him an accusing look, her chest rising and falling. Then she moved down the hall toward the bedroom. In a moment he heard the door close hard.

Art leaned back, felt a week's worth of fatigue settle into his back and shoulders. After a while he stood and flipped off the light. The milk-white moon hung framed in the window above the sink. All he wanted to do was collapse on a mattress and lie perfectly still, but instead he stepped outside, shuffling to the edge of the backyard where he leaned against one of the shortleaf pines. Above him the moon loomed low, reminding him of stories old people used to tell of moonlight falling on the marriage bed, stories holding hope of blessings and children nine months on.

Blessings had come, surely. There had been good days on the river and in the deer woods, first with Bobby, then David. Or when Bobby grew old enough to take a place on the crew and custom houses went up, one or two a year.

But Art hadn't credited Bobby's impatience, his frustration at building fine houses without owning one himself. Bobby's work turned haphazard then, and Art let him go to teach a lesson he thought would stick. Instead Bobby left for Jonesboro. They'd hardly spoken since.

Art felt tightness spreading in his back, so he moved toward the pergola he'd hired David to build last winter, when the boy first joined the crew. February had been a slow month, and he'd figured David could use the money. The pergola made Ann Marie proud as a peach, but Art remembered being disappointed in the work. Now he gave each corner post a shake, testing for firmness, noting some give in the braces above. The length and angle of the 2x4's seemed right, but David probably hadn't used long enough deck screws. Plus the ledges on two of the planter boxes seemed loose. Groaning, Art got down on his knees to examine one of the planters more closely, testing the workmanship as if he were a blind man trying to retrace the motions of his grandson's hands. At least David had done well with the butt-joints at each corner, and the trim pieces seemed tight.

To relieve his knees, Art sat in the grass and leaned against the planter box, hearing the wood creak a bit as it took his weight. The give in the pergola's angled braces lodged a burr in his brain that wouldn't go away, shoddiness crying out for attention. He told himself another fix-it job would merely lengthen his to-do list, and now that his crew was short a man he'd have less time than ever for home repairs. He sat a while and stewed, suddenly recalling with a start that Ann Marie's seventieth birthday was only a couple of weeks away. Sighing, he calculated the long odds David might return for a celebration dinner. He decided the odds were even longer in Bobby's case, and Ann Marie would be too stubborn to ask for herself. She'd insist Art smooth feathers on his own—though he was hopeless at such things, no clue where to start. Discouraged, he raised rough palms to his eyes and tried to massage away fatigue. Eventually a scene of David and Bobby helping him repair the pergola formed in his mind. He couldn't imagine so unlikely a circumstance coming about, but he sat for a long time with his back against the planter, letting the picture linger.

# FOUR FINE HORSES

I never thought I'd set foot on this property again, but here I am at the back of the crowd in my father's sale barn, watching Trent Tilson show a good Foxtrotter mare. He rides her bareback so we'll see how bridle-wise she is, and her colt trails at her heels like a hound. The mare ribbons around the ring in a gliding gait bred here in the Ozarks, and Trent sits her so well I can't spot daylight between his tailbone and her spine. There's no bounce, no movement in him at all.

Off to the side Trent's father, Paul, is working hard. "You'll not see a gentler mare all day," he calls into the microphone. "You can saddle her right out of the pasture. Plus that pretty colt. Two for the price of one."

I watch Paul's eyes rake the crowd. He has a solid bid but he looks insulted, thinks the mare's worth more. "Come on now," he shouts, his microphone booming like something dropped from the sky. "Look how smooth she is. Trent's gone to sleep up there."

Trent cracks a little grin, letting us know he heard the joke. Then his face goes stony again.

To my left, an old man has been sitting cross-armed all morning, but now he gives one hand a flick, not much more than a tremor. Paul nods and his voice changes from pleading to pleased. The bid rises another ten dollars, stays there for several more minutes. Gradually the crowd becomes as still as the air. "Are you done?" Paul shouts. He lifts an open hand to us as the mare and colt swing in a circle behind him. I listen to the steady drumming of hooves. Finally he drops his hand. "She's sold," he intones, and the crowd sighs.

In the center of the ring the mare slows to a walk. Trent goes loose of limb, his heels dangling below her girth. Beside me, the old man re-balances a Tindle feed cap, reaches inside his windbreaker for a tiny notepad. He scribbles something in a dull hand, then gets up and goes. The next thing he writes will be a check to my father.

I hardly knew the place this morning. It was never what you'd associate with some of those Thoroughbred operations in Kentucky—clean white fences, pastures cropped as close as fairways—but it looks pretty good for an Arkansas hill farm, which is all it was twenty years ago when Mom and I left. I spent four summers with my father after that, but one day when I was fourteen I told him I was through. He could've made me stay, we both knew that, but all he did was nod his head.

From what I could see driving in, the woods have been cleared, and there are three barns now. One of them, the sale barn, stretches across a good part of the south ridge, and where the hill levels out there's a long flat field with just a few oaks and cedars. People use that field to park, and I saw plates this morning from all over—Missouri, Oklahoma, Kansas.

I saw the sign too, the big blue one above the entrance to the sale barn that read Cecil Ryan Stables. It slowed me down for a step or two, and I didn't know why until I remembered the other sign, the hand-lettered one he supposedly nailed to the rack of his pickup the week I was born. That one read Ryan & Son: Registered Quarter Horses.

I guess I came this morning because of Trent, who's trying to pass my Comp course at the college. The kid's pretty much a lost soul with a pen in his hand, no confidence that he has anything to say or any way to say it. A couple of weeks ago I hauled him into my office and set a full cup of coffee in front of him. It was black and bad, but he took the first sip without complaining. "You're having some trouble," I said. "You think maybe you're trying too hard?"

His hand was a little unsteady, and he spilled just enough coffee to darken the dust on one of his boots. "You're the first teacher's ever accused me of that."

"No harm in being the first."

"I guess not."

I waited for him to look up from his coffee, or the floor, whatever he was staring at.

When he didn't, I flipped through my grade book. "Well, what are we going to do? You're not passing."

He nodded, and I could see the shape of his skull beneath his buzz cut. "I guess I better drop," he said.

I've been teaching six years now, two as a TA at Fayetteville, four as an adjunct at ASU. Here this kid was flunking a freshman course at Ozark Mountain Community College. It should have been an easy call to agree with him, tell him dropping was the best thing, but I decided to try. "Your boots," I said. "They Justins?"

He looked up then, shook his head. "Noconas."

"I always liked Justins."

Half a smile came on his face, like he didn't know whether to smirk or grin. Finally the grin won, but he still looked at me out of the corner of his eye. "One of those city cowboys, huh?"

I had to laugh. "No, no kind of cowboy. My dad had a horse farm though. Still does, I guess. Over in Stevis."

A light spread in his eyes, like he might be putting my last name together with my father's. We talked a little easier after that, and eventually he told me he and his dad worked most of the horse sales in North Arkansas, including every one Cecil Ryan held. Teaching is catch-as-catch-can, so I tried again. "Why don't you write about work," I said. "Something about horses."

He took a quick glimpse at the door, then brought his eyes back to mine. "I wouldn't know what to say."

I took a sip of my coffee, decided I might as well roll the dice. "Why not? Don't you know anything about horses?"

His jaw went hard as he studied me. "You know anything about teaching?"

"I guess I'm trying to find out."

Paul calls another rider into the ring now, a heavy-set man on a good-looking red mare. Paul says the man is showing her as a favor to his daughter, that he's driven all the way from Hot Springs because we know Foxtrotters here. The man slides off and jogs the mare around the ring a few times to let us see her action, then grabs the horn and swings himself back into the saddle. He's not smooth like Trent, and he has some trouble gaining his stirrups again. The mare senses him struggling and breaks stride, bolts a little to the side so that she's no longer moving in the tight circle the man wants. Frustrated, he gets rough with the bit trying to muscle her back in line, and she takes a quick little hop beneath him. A good six inches flash between his crotch and the saddle, and he comes down high in the seat. He tries to grin it off, like he and the mare do this every day for fun, but the grin is tighter than a clothesline.

Paul's been pretty quiet so far, but now he decides he ought to turn storyteller. "This man's daughter hurt her back," he says, "but he's doing what he can to help her. He needs a fair bid on this mare, and she's worth it. You'll be getting her at the good price of a daddy's love. We'll start her at $300. Let me hear you now. Let me hear."

Nobody will go near that price though. The man takes turn after turn around the ring, and each time he looks more frustrated. Finally he reins the mare back on her haunches and slides off in the middle of the ring. He reaches beneath her and loosens the girth strap, then lets the saddle drop to the ground. At first I think he's going to lead her off, but instead he hops on bareback the way Trent did and starts riding with his heels. The mare doesn't like it, and every few strides she gives a little buck.

Paul hustles into the middle of the ring now, trying to get the man's attention. "What's your low price?" he calls. "What'll you let her go for?"

The man takes a last trip around the ring, glaring at Paul the whole time. He heels the mare in close, and when he dismounts it looks for a second like there may be trouble. Instead, he shoulders his saddle and leads the mare off on a short rein. A few steps outside the ring she jerks her head hard, nearly lifting him off his feet. A ripple of laughter skips through the crowd, and Paul hurries in a new horse.

This morning when I passed beneath that blue sign I actually held my breath. I guess I half expected my father to be there at the door. Several people were pushing up behind me, so I moved on and took a seat in one of the metal folding chairs at the end of the back row. I realized then that I wanted to spot him before he saw me. That way I could decide whether to go up to him or not, whether to say anything or just walk out and drive away, no harm no foul.

I did phone him once after I took the job at Ozark Mountain, basically just to let him know. I got the answering machine and left my number. That night he called while I was in class and left his number, even though I already had it. I played the message back a couple of times, trying to match his voice with the one I remembered in my head. Finally I did, and I cleared the message.

When I was a little boy, I sometimes sat on the floor beside my father's desk and listened to him think of potential names for the new foals. At first he'd sound the names out as if they were words from a foreign tongue, his voice moving slowly through the syllables—Acie's Lad, Carter's Con, Piddling Pride—until he was sure of each name's rightness. Then he'd repeat the name four or five times, each repetition firmer and louder, until the name sounded as if he'd used it all his life.

My favorite was the one he gave to a pretty bay mare, Pappy's Cat. She had a bit of Poco Bueno blood, which meant she went back to a foundation sire, but all I cared about was the brightness of her coat when the sun hit it just right and the fact that she would nuzzle my face when the other mares wouldn't. One morning in late spring, when I was six, I left the house alone to go looking for her. The way I remember it, I made my way toward the line of trees that marked the beginning of the far pasture. By the time I got there I'd begun to wonder whether I should have come that far, but the small stand of oak thinned and opened before me, showing the deep scoop of the pond bank in the distance. Beyond the pond another line of oaks floated in a shimmer of fog that curled among the trunks and silvered the higher branches caught in the sun. I went toward them, soaking my jeans in the tall, dewy grass, even becoming a little chilled. Then, before I saw, I knew. A hoof scraped across a stone. Moments later a deep burst of breath rode the air somewhere near me, almost readying me for the sudden swelling of her head and neck as she loomed hugely out of the fog.

I stumbled backward, my concentration held by the blaze face and the long black forelock, and then the huge eyes erupting out of the forehead as fiercely as fists. Suddenly she swung her head away, curling her neck toward the leggy dark colt tripping at her hindquarters. A narrow blaze ran down his face and widened in a strange pool of whiteness about his nostrils. I moved forward, trying to touch that blaze, but she wheeled and fronted me, her hooves rasping the stony ground. Frozen, I smelled her, the salt-thick odor of horses, and then my father lifted me by the collar, holding me out and away at the end of his extended arm. With the other he waved her off before carrying me clear of the trees, his fist still balling my collar till I thought I would choke.

Halfway to the pond he set me down in the wet grass, letting me cough all I needed to before leaning his face close to mine. "Why?" he said. "Tell me why?"

I didn't know what he was asking. Dark stubble covered his face, and I remembered how the whiskers would prick my palms when I slid my hands across his jaws. I shook my head.

He looked back at the trees and pointed in their direction. "She just foaled," he said. "You've got to wait till that foal is bigger."

I probably nodded, or mumbled "yessir," anything to convince him I understood, but what has remained clearest in my memory is a moment late that night when I woke to feel his big hand spread flat on my chest. He was leaning over me, his weight coming down through his hand so that I could hear the bedsprings beneath me. "Rick," he was saying. "I'm sorry. Don't hold it against me."

◆   ◆   ◆

Trent seems to be on a break. Another rider has shown the last few horses, and my chair is getting hard. I slip outside, where the field below the barn is dotted with vehicles, everything from truck and trailer rigs to a Honda Civic. There are plenty of spots though, because the horse market is down. I imagine most of the people here have come just to see horses, or each other.

West of the barn is a metal training ring where several people are gathered. I wander over to watch the only rider, a boy—maybe eleven or twelve—on a gray roan. The mare shows a smooth gait, clay flicking steadily from her hooves. To me she looks like a fine horse, but one of the men isn't pleased. He keeps shouting directions to the boy, trying to get him to sit straight-backed, to shorten the reins and hold them lower down, near his belt buckle. The boy looks like he's trying, but he's tentative. After a trip or two around the ring he's hunching over the pommel, both hands clutching the reins to his chest.

After a while the man draws my attention. He may be the boy's father, but he's fully gray, with leathery lines in his face and neck. His jeans hang slack about his rear, and he wears one of those wide belts with his name, Cochran, stamped into the leather. His agitation keeps building, and finally he scrambles into the ring, coming at the mare from the side. She spots him and shies, bolting so hard she nearly unseats the rider. The boy loses both reins and a stirrup, and if it weren't for the saddle horn he'd be in the dirt.

Several men scale the metal railing, and a couple drop into the ring, but it's Cochran who gets to the horse, his left hand reaching for the boy, his right seeking out the reins. Suddenly there's a surge of motion, man and boy caught in a struggle with a fractious mare. Eventually Cochran gets hold of the headstall and calms her enough that she comes to a stop, though she stands walleyed and trembling. The boy has both legs on the mare's off side, one foot wedged awkwardly in the stirrup. Cochran has to support him, holding him about the waist while the boy tries to work his way loose. "Damn it," Cochran growls. "I told you not to wear those flat-heeled boots." The boy's face blooms red, and he nearly kicks the mare in extricating himself. When Cochran sets him on the ground, he jerks away angrily. "Hey now," Cochran shouts, his voice like a pistol shot, and the boy stops in his tracks. He stands there with his head lowered, his hands fisted, while Cochran talks to the mare, slowly coaxing her toward the gate. As they get closer one of the men eases it open, and Cochran turns back, offering the reins to the boy. The kid's face is still fever-red, but he wants those reins. Taking them in both hands, he walks the mare through, matching his father's slow, careful pace.

As they pass, I hear the boy's loud breathing and realize how intently I'm listening, trying to catch anything father or son might say.

All these years I've kept a little 3x3 snapshot of the house before it burned. I think I took it from the album my mother packed away at the back of a closet in her parents' house in Fayetteville. The photo shows a corner of the barn and paddock in the foreground, with a side view of the house and white rail fence behind. Everything looks fresh and clean, almost restful, nothing like the soot and ash that my mother, angered beyond action, refused to sift through.

What I remember most about that day is not the smoke or flames coming through the barn roof, but rather the sight of my father running along the fence row, our border collie racing near his legs. I'd been playing in the yard, but everything seemed to stop as I watched him run. Suddenly his boot sole slipped on a loose stone and he went down so quickly he couldn't get his arms extended in front of him. By the time he rose—still running, his legs never stopped moving—a dull redness had bled through the sleeves of his white shirt.

My eyes were still on the redness when he ran past me toward the house. He shouted, and when I turned I saw my mother appear behind the screen door. She pushed it open and stepped halfway onto the porch. One hand still gripped the door handle, but the other rose in the air as if she were trying to ward flames from the barn away from the house. When she saw me in the side yard she ran, her teal shorts flashing above the white tennis shoes and the short white socks, and in the next moment I was running with her in the ditch beside the road. We were nearly a hundred yards from the house when she jerked me to a stop and thrust her face near mine. "You stay here," she shouted. "Don't set foot in that yard." I didn't follow her all the way, but I went close enough to watch her return to the yard and scream at my father's back, trying to get him to leave the wild-eyed mares in the paddock and help her wet down the roof of the house. He just waved her away, chasing the mares to the far end of the pasture while my mother sank to her knees and watched wind whip the flames onto the roof of our house. When neighbors arrived with shovels and buckets, she was weeping in the ditch next to the gate, her face streaked with smoke and mascara. The next day she moved the two of us into her parents' house in Fayetteville, and she never went back.

The training ring isn't that far from where the house burned, although the ground is rough. It won't take me long to walk, but I doubt there will be anything to see. That first summer I spent with my father, when I was eleven, he bulldozed whatever was left into the cellar and covered it over with dirt that still looked charred. There might be a few volunteer trees growing out of it now, but nothing else.

Turning back to the barn, I catch sight of Trent at the side entrance. He's helping someone check in a small string of paint ponies, but I can tell he spots me. When he finishes with the horses, I go up and give him a nod.

"Been wondering if you'd come," he says.

"I keep a naturally low profile."

He laughs. "A man can't be too careful."

"That's what I hear."

He bangs a heel on the toe of the other boot, raising dust. "So you grew up on this place?"

"Mainly summers."

Nodding, he chews a piece of straw for a while. "It's pretty. I wouldn't mind having something like it someday. It's a tough go now, though."

"Eat your Wheaties."

"No kidding. Big bowl every meal."

This time I laugh. Looking around, I ask, "How's the essay coming? You think you can find any material?"

His head doesn't drop the way it usually does. Instead, he works the straw to the corner of his mouth and hikes his shoulders a little as he leans against the door. "Well, I'm bettin' the ladies at the Writing Center are tired of me."

"Putting them to work, huh?"

"Or them me."

"That's what it takes."

He rolls his eyes a little, but I can tell he secretly agrees, like a man who's finally faced down something he dreaded. "Bring it by the office," I tell him. "We'll give it a look."

"Yeah, that sounds good." He stretches a bit, showing his wingspan, then hooks a thumb toward the barn's interior. "Better go ride some ponies," he says.

I give him a mock salute. As he leaves I step closer to the door so I can watch him work. At the holding pen a tall, round-bellied man with a clipboard pulls him aside and points out something about one of the paints. Trent nods and enters the pen. The older man glances briefly at the open door where I stand, then looks again, startled. I see he's grown a mustache now, white and neatly trimmed. I step away and close the door.

That final summer, things were pretty bad. I was about to start high school in Fayetteville, and the last place I wanted to be was some horse farm in Bond County. My father had spent his share of the insurance money building his first barn, and what little was left went toward payments on a used house trailer I called the Tin Can. It had one air conditioner that blew the same weak stream no matter what the setting, and the bathroom was so small I once banged my head on the sink trying to dry my legs after a shower.

The worst part was the work. Maybe I was lazy, but it felt like the only reason he wanted me there during the summers was to bend my back. He paid for the food, let me fold out the couch at night, so any minute I wasn't eating or sleeping was free labor. I walked miles behind his baler, throwing sixty and seventy pound bales onto the flatbed and knowing with every toss that the hardest part was still to come, the suffocating hay loft in some farmer's barn where each bale had to be hauled and stacked by hand. Or on the days when he made extra cash driving a truck for Reeves Hardware, I had to cut sprouts and dig postholes on the back twenty, because he wanted to cross-fence it and use it as another hayfield. I probably could have stood it if he'd let me work with the horses a little more than he did, but he was already starting to train and stable some of the better show horses in the area, and he didn't have time for me to learn on the job.

The blow-up came on a Sunday morning in late July. We'd hauled from six till dusk the day before, and I had a copy of *A Separate Peace* I'd been waiting to read all summer. A girl I liked in Fayetteville had let me borrow it, and I'd decided today was the day. I was about ten pages into it, stretched out on the couch and still in my underwear, when he came in from the barn.

"What are you doing?" he said.

I stared at the ceiling. "What's it look like?"

"You're not up yet?"

I held the book toward his face so he could see the cover.

"You can do that later."

I looked at him then, saw that his shirt and jeans were already dusty. "Later don't come here," I said.

He stiffened, the way I'd seen him do with an uncooperative horse. "Get up, Rick."

"I'm going to read this book."

His quickness startled me, the open hand slapping the book away like a scythe blade topping a sprout. The book landed on the dirty dishes in the kitchen sink and I thought of Holly Sanders, her soft cheeks and sweet-smelling hair. I'd never hit him but I tried, and when he blocked the punch I dropped my shoulder into his chest, counting on leg strength to drive him out the door. Twice he threw me back against the couch, but the third time he grabbed hold and we wrestled our way onto the stoop, where he slung me over the flimsy railing and into the yard. I sat up, but I didn't charge him again. He stepped close and stood over me. "You can get dressed or you can come like that."

"Or I can leave," I said.

He took a funny-sounding breath, like maybe one of my punches had had a delayed effect, and I watched his shoulders slump a little as he looked out over what passed as a yard. I kept waiting for him to say something, but he never did. Finally he set his jaw, nodded, and walked off toward the barn.

At the start of every summer my mother gave me enough money for bus fare back to Fayetteville, saying, "Don't be afraid to use it." The moment he left for the barn I went back in and cleaned Holly's book as best I could. Then I changed out of my grass-stained underwear and shoved what clothes I'd brought into my duffle bag. I hiked and hitched the nine miles into Lotten, where I sat at the bus stop for three hours before catching the ride home.

I was right about the trees. A little stand has volunteered here, mainly cedar and wild peach. The rest of what used to be the yard and paddock is fenced off into pasture, and to the west a few mares are grazing on the far ridge. I half expected this place to feel like a cemetery, but there is too little left of what had been. Maybe that makes it easier for him, if it was ever hard.

I follow the patchy remains of the drive down to the county road, and that's when I see him. His shoulders are half-turned, like he can't decide whether to come on up or go back. The sale is still going, so I'm stunned he left to follow me. The old drive is the only path through the weeds though, so I move down to where he's standing.

"Pretty big turnout," I say.

He's studying my face, the way somebody will who hasn't seen you in a long time, but I'm doing the same to him, noticing the blotch of brown spots at the top of his cheekbones. From the sun, I guess.

"Nobody's buying though," he says, and nods toward the homeplace. "Come back to see?"

"Something like that."

He smoothes his mustache with the back of his thumb. "So you're teaching now?"

I nod. "Trent's one of my students."

"I heard that. He's a good kid."

"Seems to be."

"He can sure sit a horse. Better than I ever could."

"I saw him. He's smooth."

"He sure is."

My father tests his lower lip with his teeth, and I'm struck by how white they still are beneath the white mustache. He seems to want to say something, and after a moment he reaches out and taps me on the chest with his open palm. "I know you hold a lot against me," he says. "No way to keep from it."

The hand is withdrawn, but I can feel its imprint, the quick, strong warmth of its weight. "We do what we can," I say.

He's still testing his lip. "I guess so," he says, and looks down, scraping the sparse gravel with his toe. After a moment he raises his head and makes a clicking sound with his tongue and cheek, like he's urging a horse into a canter. "Gotta get back," he says, though he doesn't move.

I stand here knowing I should say something, but my mind is blank. Finally he starts to turn, and I hold out my hand.

He takes it, seems grateful for it, and heads back toward the sale barn. When he's almost out of sight I notice the mares have started down off the ridge, making their way toward him as if they expect him to come to the fence and feed them sugar from his palm—four fine horses, all bays, the noon sun bright on their backs.

C. D. ALBIN was born and reared in West Plains, Missouri. He earned a Doctor of Arts in English from the University of Mississippi and has taught for many years at Missouri State University–West Plains, where he founded and edits *Elder Mountain: A Journal of Ozarks Studies.* His stories, poems, and reviews have appeared in a number of periodicals, including *Arkansas Review, Cape Rock, Georgia Review, Harvard Review, Natural Bridge,* and *Slant.*

Cover artist DAWN D. SURRATT studied art at the University of North Carolina at Greensboro as a recipient of the Spencer Love Scholarship in Fine Art. She has exhibited her work throughout the Southeast and currently works as a freelance designer and artist. Her work has been published internationally in magazines, on book covers, and in print media. She lives on the beautiful Kerr Lake in northern North Carolina with her husband, one demanding cat, and a crazy Pembroke Welsh Corgi.

www.ingramcontent.com/pod-product-compliance
Lightning Source LLC
Chambersburg PA
CBHW020643250626
47154CB00008B/2794